KV-687-684

FRANKIE'S ROMEO

Ruth Louise Symes

TED SMART

First published in Great Britain in 2002
as a Dolphin paperback
by Orion Children's Books
a division of the Orion Publishing Group Ltd
Orion House
5 Upper St Martin's Lane
London WC2H 9EA

Text copyright © Ruth Louise Symes 2002

The right of Ruth Louise Symes to be identified
as the author of this work has been asserted.

All rights reserved. No part of this publication may be
reproduced, stored in a retrieval system, or transmitted,
in any form or by any means, electronic, mechanical,
photocopying, recording, or otherwise, without the prior
permission of Orion Children's Books.

This edition produced for
The Book People Ltd
Hall Wood Avenue,
Haydock,
St Helens WA11 9UL

A catalogue record for this book is
available from the British Library

Typeset at The Spartan Press Ltd,
Lymington, Hants

Printed in Great Britain by
Clays Ltd, St Ives plc

ISBN 1 84255 086 1

It was freezing on the hockey pitch. Ice crystals shone on the ends of Frankie's spiky short brown hair. Miserably she stared down at her raw pink knees, then crossed her eyes to try and squint at her nose to see which was the pinker. The PE kit Miss Myers had given her from the lost property box felt itchy. She hoped whoever had worn it last hadn't had fleas. At her old school if you didn't have a PE kit you had to sit out and watch. But not at Brentfield.

'Wake up, goalie!' yelled bossy Leanne, making Frankie jump.

Harriet, the captain of the other side, had got the ball and was tearing down the field like one of the space monsters from *Kookie the Space Warrior*.

Leanne ran in to tackle, but Harriet knocked her out of her way and Leanne landed on the muddy ground.

'Ow!'

Frankie gulped as Harriet charged onwards towards the goal she was supposed to be defending.

Wendy, Leanne's best friend, dropped her hockey stick and ran over to help Leanne up.

Harriet was almost at the goal.

Frankie had to do something!

She leapt to the left as Harriet whacked the ball into the right-hand corner of the net with such force that it almost went through it.

'Phew! That was close.'

The hockey pitch erupted with groans from Frankie's team and cheers from Harriet's.

'Upsadaisy,' Wendy said, trying to pull Leanne to her feet. Leanne looked daggers at her, pushed her hand away and struggled to her feet unaided, slipping in the mud as she did so. She noticed some of the other girls watching her.

'What d'you think you're looking at?'

The girls quickly looked away. Leanne brushed at the mud on her previously pristine PE kit.

'This top is ruined,' she shouted at Frankie. 'It's all your fault.'

'My fault?' Frankie squeaked back.

'Yeah, you're not even trying,' Wendy told her.

'Yes I am. We didn't play hockey at my old school.'

'Didn't play hockey at my old school,' Leanne repeated, in a supposed-to-be-funny imitation of Frankie's voice. 'Well, even an idiot knows a goalkeeper's supposed to stop goals. We're bound to lose now, thanks to you.'

'Sorry I'm sure. Not,' Frankie muttered to herself.

The PE teacher, Miss Myers, blew the whistle.

'Well played, Harriet. Back to your places everyone.'

Frankie opened her mouth and stuck out her bottom lip to direct hot air up to her icy nose. Didn't Miss Myers feel the cold? Probably not. Anyway, she was wearing a tracksuit and a fleece, leggings, scarf, gloves, and a hat over her shaved head.

Frankie wished for the zillionth time that afternoon that she could be back at her old school, doing aerobics in the warm studio instead of hockey in the cold. She'd been at Brentfield for two weeks and so far it hadn't been any fun at all.

Meera ran over to Miss Myers. 'Please, miss, can I go to the loo?' she asked, her long black hair blowing across her face. She crossed her legs and jumped about a bit.

Miss Myers frowned. 'But you've been twice already.'

Meera hopped up and down some more. 'I know miss. Me mam says I've got a weak bladder.'

'Well I don't see why you've only got one in PE,' Miss Myers said, and blew the whistle again. 'You can wait till after the game.'

'But miss,' Meera wailed.

'Oh for goodness sake, go on then.'

Frankie smiled at Meera, but Meera didn't notice. She was grinning to herself as she ran off the pitch. Frankie wished she'd thought of saying she needed the loo too.

'Ninety seconds left, girls,' Miss Myers said. 'You're one man down now, Harriet, so I'll play on your team.'

'Right. Concentrate,' Frankie told herself.

Miss Myers blew the whistle and started dribbling the ball down the pitch. 'Come on! Stop me, stop me!' she shouted.

Harriet might have been like a space monster from an episode of *Kookie the Space Warrior* but Miss Myers was more like a nimble space sprite. Some of the girls half-heartedly ran in to tackle her but she weaved around them easily.

Frankie bit her bottom lip. 'Mustn't forget wind resistance . . . estimated ball arrival time fifteen seconds.'

Miss Myers focused on the net. Frankie focused on Miss Myers.

'This is it . . . Focus, Frankie . . . Two seconds! Now!'

Frankie dived out of the way as the ball slammed into the back of the net. The mud she landed in was fortunately squelchy rather than hard. It had been thawed a bit by the many hockey boots that had run through it during the afternoon.

Harriet's team went crazy, cheering and congratulating each other like mad.

Frankie's team didn't go crazy. Some of them looked at Frankie with distaste. Some of them shook their heads. The mud beneath Frankie felt squelchy and cold but she hadn't been hit by the ball. Not even once, during the whole afternoon. Well done, Frankie.

'You're useless, Frankie,' Wendy said.

'We should never have picked you for our team,' said Leanne.

'Sorry,' Frankie said. Although she didn't really feel sorry. Wendy and Leanne had made it clear that she was only on their team because Miss Myers had said they had to have her. She was the goalkeeper because no one else wanted to be.

Slowly Frankie stood up.

Miss Myers blew her whistle. 'Game over. 5-0.'

Two frozen hockey teams stumbled off the pitch towards the changing rooms.

The winning team stumbled triumphantly. The losing team didn't.

Miss Myers jogged over to Frankie. 'Try to make more of an effort next time, Frankie. It's trying that counts, you know.' She jogged off, calling, 'Try to try harder.'

Try harder? Frankie thought as she trailed after everyone else to get changed. Didn't Miss Myers know how hard it was to avoid being hit by a speeding hockey ball?

Meera was already dressed by the time everyone had bundled into the changing room. She was sitting on a bench, chewing gum.

'You're not chewing, are you, Meera?' Miss Myers said.

Meera immediately swallowed it and said in an innocent voice, 'No, miss.'

'Models never chew gum, you know – they don't want to end up with fat muscly faces.'

'I don't want to be a model, miss.'

Miss Myers sighed and disappeared into her small office at one end of the changing room. Frankie sank onto a bench. Was there anything worse than playing hockey on a cold Friday afternoon? Probably not.

Leanne and Wendy were getting changed next to her.

'It's your fault we lost, Frankie,' Wendy said.

Frankie ignored her. The main thing was she was alive and unmarked by a hockey ball. She'd survived the ordeal. Also, she was new to the school and had no one to stick up for her, so it was best not to retaliate. Much better to concentrate on getting dressed.

Leanne helped herself to a lipgloss from Wendy's fluffy makeup bag.

'Mm, strawberry, my favourite.'

Wendy scowled at her. 'That's mine . . . you could ask. Just once.'

'Share and share alike.'

'Yeah, but it's always my things we're sharing,' said Wendy.

Leanne looked closely at her chin in the mirror.

'D'you think I'm getting a spot?'

'No, you look fine, as always,' Wendy said grumpily. 'Mirror, mirror on the wall, Leanne's the fairest of them all.'

Frankie smirked and Leanne scowled at her, then turned to Wendy. 'I'm not having Frankie on my team again, no matter what Myers says.'

'No, she's totally useless,' Wendy agreed, as she reapplied glitter shadow to her eyelids. They smiled at each other.

'It's not like it was the World Cup,' Frankie muttered. She was already dressed and had her head bent over the exercise book she was writing in. The next second the book was ripped from her and Frankie had drawn a jagged line across the page.

'Hey, give that back!' Frankie shouted.

But Leanne didn't give it back. 'What are you doing, anyway,' she said. 'Writing love letters?' She winked at Wendy, then looked at the book and sighed. 'Oh no – she's doing her science homework. What a goody-goody.'

'Yeah and now you've made me mess it up,' Frankie said, trying to get her book back.

'Bor-ing,' said Wendy.

'No it isn't,' Frankie told her. 'I really liked making that wormery – just because you were scared of a few little worms.' She reached for her book but Leanne climbed onto a bench and held it above her head.

'Give it back,' Frankie said.

'Nope.'

'I suppose you like worms because you are one,' Wendy said.

'D'you know something – you're really thick, Wendy!'

'And you're really ugly!' said Leanne and she threw the book across the changing room and came at Frankie with Wendy's lipgloss. 'Let's see if we can improve you a bit.'

'Getoff!' Frankie said, pushing her away. 'I don't want that muck on my face.'

'Huh, bet she's never had a boyfriend,' Wendy said.

'Who'd want to go out with her?' said Leanne.

Wendy and Leanne laughed.

'You're pathetic,' Frankie said and went to get her book before they could see how much they'd upset her.

Miss Myers came out of her office. She'd changed into jeans and a sweatshirt.

'Hurry up and get changed girls. Wendy, if you put on any more makeup you'll look like a clown.'

'Yes, miss,' said Wendy. She poked her tongue out at Miss Myers as she disappeared back into her office.

Frankie found her book under a bench near Meera.

'Just ignore them – they're only trying to wind you up,' Meera whispered.

'Well, they're doing a good job,' Frankie said. She went back to Leanne and Wendy, holding the book close to her chest. 'For your information, science is a thousand times more important than a silly game of hockey!' she told them.

'Huh?' said Wendy.

'Mad,' said Leanne.

But Frankie didn't take it back. Science was her favourite subject. She'd come top in her class at her old school and top in the science test today. One day she wanted to be a scientist, like her gran had been before she retired.

'And another thing,' said Frankie.

'What?' said Leanne.

'I have got one – so there.'

'Only one?' said Leanne.

'What are you talking about, Frankie?' said Wendy.

'A boyfriend. I do have one.'

'Oh yeah,' said Leanne, smiling knowingly. 'What's his name then?'

For a second Frankie couldn't think. Then she stammered, 'Er – er, Romeo.'

'Romeo!' Wendy and Leanne screeched. A few of the other girls, who'd been pretending not to be listening, smiled to themselves. It was too late for Frankie to think of another name. Everyone had heard. Better make the best of it.

'Yes, Romeo.'

'You made him up,' said Wendy.

Leanne finished putting on her mascara. 'I bet I know where she got that name from.'

'Where?' said Wendy. And Frankie almost asked

where as well. The name had just popped into her head.

'You know that film,' Leanne said, and started waving her arms around and over-acting badly, 'Romeo, Romeo, wherefore art thou Romeo?'

'He's not Leonardo diCaprio, stupid,' Frankie said.

'OK – what's this Romeo of yours look like? If he really exists,' Wendy said.

'He . . . er . . . he.'

Luckily Miss Myers came out of her office. 'Haven't you girls gone yet? Go on, out you go – now!'

Everyone bundled out, shooed along like geese by Miss Myers.

Frankie hid in the loos until she was sure Leanne and Wendy must have gone. This was a disaster. What was she going to do? Why did she say she had a boyfriend? How could she have been so stupid? No one was ever going to like her if she was branded a liar.

Eventually she came out of the loos, only to find Leanne and Wendy waiting for her.

'I've got a photo of my boyfriend,' Wendy said, pulling a photo of a boy from her bag.

'And I've got a photo of mine,' said Leanne. 'Where's your photo of your boyfriend, Frankie?'

'I – I've not got it with me,' Frankie said, wishing they'd just leave her alone.

'I bet you haven't,' said Leanne sarcastically.

'But I have got one,' Frankie insisted.

'Seeing is believing,' said Wendy.

'Yeah, it is, so bring a photo of him to school on Monday – so we can see what he looks like,' Leanne said.

'All right, I will!' said Frankie, and finally they left her alone.

'What am I going to do?' she thought desperately, as she walked out of the school gates. Her big mouth had landed her in trouble before but never as bad as this. If she didn't produce a photograph of a boyfriend on Monday morning then everyone was going to know she'd lied, and even though she knew lying was wrong and never pays – because you always get found out in the end – it didn't make her look forward to getting found out.

'Hey, Frankie!' a voice called after her, but Frankie ignored it. She didn't want to talk to anyone. All she'd wanted was to be the same as the other girls. To be liked by them. To make just one friend and be accepted. And now she'd ended up in this mess.

'Hey Frankie, wait up!' the voice shouted again.

Frankie stopped.

Darren came running up, his overloaded bag swinging behind him.

'Hi,' he gasped, his dark cheeks flushed. Darren was in the same year as Frankie but not in the same form. He lived round the corner and always seemed to be about whenever she was walking to or from school. Darren's dad was the science teacher at Brentfield. His mum was a science teacher too but at another school.

'Hi, Darren,' Frankie said.

They started walking together. Frankie hoped Darren hadn't heard about the boyfriend discussion in the girls' changing room. But of course he had.

'Is it true?'

'What?'

'Do you have a boyfriend called Romeo?'

Frankie sighed.

'You didn't tell me you had a boyfriend.'

'I . . .'

'What's he like?'

Darren didn't sound excited about her imaginary boyfriend, he sounded sad.

Maybe he's sad because he thinks I should have told him before, Frankie thought. But why should he care if she had a boyfriend or not?

'No, it isn't true,' Frankie admitted. 'It was a total lie.'

'Frankie . . .'

'I know, I know. It wasn't deliberate – Wendy and Leanne made me so cross the lie just slipped out, and then got bigger and bigger and everyone was listening, and Wendy was smirking, and I just couldn't take the lie back, I couldn't.'

'I see.'

'Huh – that's not all. Now I have to produce a photo of me and Romeo by Monday morning and if I don't then everyone will know I lied and don't really have a boyfriend and no one will ever like me. I just don't know what I'm going to do. My life's a disaster.'

Frankie looked over at Darren. He was smiling! Didn't he appreciate the seriousness of what had happened? The mess she was in?

'What are you looking so happy about?' Frankie asked. She didn't feel like smiling. She felt like crying. Crying a lot.

'Oh nothing,' Darren said.

'So what d'you think I should do?'

Darren was quiet for a bit. Then: 'Well, you could say you've broken up with Romeo and are now going out with someone from Brentfield instead.'

Someone from school! 'Are you mad, Darren? No one from school wants to go out with me.'

'I . . .' Darren started to say, but Frankie interrupted him.

'And I certainly don't want to go out with anyone from Brentfield. Yuk!'

Darren sighed and then shrugged. 'You'll think of something, Frankie.'

They'd reached the corner where Darren had to go one way and Frankie had to go the other.

'Don't worry. See you at school on Monday,' Darren said and walked off.

'Not if I can catch chickenpox or a cold or anything else that'll keep me off school you won't,' Frankie called after him.

Darren disappeared down his perfectly ordinary street and Frankie turned down her almost perfectly ordinary one. The houses went: ordinary, ordinary, ordinary and then very very weird. Frankie's gran's house was the weird one. It looked like it should be in a science fiction film instead of stuck in the middle of an ordinary street. The house hadn't been weird when Frankie and her mum and dad had moved in. It had looked the same as all the other smug-looking houses. But then Frankie's dad had stuck a model of the spaceship *Enterprise* from the original *Star Trek* on the roof and placed statues of aliens in the garden and stuck a neon sign that flashed 'Science Fiction B&B' in one of the windows.

Frankie rang the front doorbell and it started playing the theme tune to *Mars Attacks* – one of the many science fiction film tunes it had on a roll.

It took ages for anyone to come. Frankie had listened to *Mars Attacks, AI* and *Close Encounters of the Third Kind* before her mum opened the door.

'Sorry, love, I was working in the studio out the back,' Mum said. Her hands were covered in bits of clay. She wiped them on her potter's apron. 'I've had a bulk order from the Convention Centre for more of those green alien figurines. The first lot sold out in just a few hours.'

'Great,' Frankie said. Mum's pottery business was starting to do really well. It was amazing how many people wanted mugs and plates with aliens on them, plus there were the vases and of course the little statues.

'Where's Dad?'

'He's upstairs working on his latest. He's probably got *The Planets* on full blast so he didn't hear the doorbell. Did you have a good day at school?'

'N . . .' Frankie started to say, but then changed it to, 'OK.' She didn't want to explain why her day had been so bad. And anyway one good thing had happened. 'Came first in the science test.'

Mum smiled. 'That's good.'

Dad came down the stairs. He was still wearing the headphones Mum insisted he wore rather than deafen her and the neighbours with the music he liked to play when he was writing.

'Hiya Frankie,' he said, and hugged her, his beard tickling her face. 'Did Mum tell you the good news?'

'Yes, more orders from the SF place.'

'And the other good news?'

'No?'

'Three people have booked to stay over the week-end.'

'We told them we weren't quite ready yet,' Mum interrupted. 'But they said they didn't mind. They're arriving at about eight o'clock this evening. Going to a science fiction weekend at the Convention Centre.'

'I told you this place would be a hit,' Dad said. 'I knew it. What do they say – location, location, location. This is the perfect place for an SF B&B.'

Frankie grinned. Maybe he was right. Maybe the place would take off and they'd earn some real money at last. She hoped so. It'd make a nice change to be able to buy things she wanted instead of always being told that there wasn't enough money. 'Please let it work out,' Frankie wished, crossing her fingers. Her mum and dad were mad about anything to do with science fiction and thought anyone who wasn't a fan would become one, once they'd read a good SF book or watched a great SF film or series on TV.

Frankie's dad spent his days trying to write science fiction short stories and novels. He dreamt of one day writing a bestseller. It was always the *next* story that was going to break through and turn him into Terry Pratchett overnight. Her mum brought in the bulk of the money, which wasn't much, with her pottery. But now there was the bed and breakfast too, which might become their biggest moneyspinner yet.

When Gran had offered them her house a little over a month ago they'd been living in a rented flat with a landlord who always complained if the rent was late. Sometimes they'd even had to pretend they weren't in when he knocked because they didn't have the money to pay him. Once they'd moved into Gran's house, and Gran had moved out, the science fiction themed B&B idea had gradually evolved. It seemed like a good idea because the Convention Centre in town regularly held SF weekends where fans went to meet the stars of and learn more about their favourite SF shows. Loads of Mum and Dad's friends, who were also SF fans, had promised to come and stay but Frankie still sometimes worried whether there'd be enough people to make the B&B profitable. But now they were having guests even before the place was officially opened. A very good sign.

'There's a postcard from your gran,' Mum said, nodding at the hall table.

Gran had given them her house when she'd decided to move in with her boyfriend, Maximilian. She'd left most of her furniture behind because there wasn't enough room for it in Maximilian's smart flat. And she'd left lots of other stuff she didn't want to take with her in boxes and trunks and on shelves down in the basement. Some of it had large labels saying 'Private' or 'Do Not Open'.

Frankie picked up the postcard. It had a picture of a giant Galapagos tortoise on the front.

Dear Frankie,

The Galapagos Islands are fascinating – did you know that there are actually 13 large islands, 16 smaller ones and 107 islets – full of amazing wildlife. We eat and sleep on board the ship so we cause as little disruption to the islands as possible. Maximilian is in his element.

Anyway, I hope you are settling in at school and that your mother and father have given up the ridiculous idea of turning my house into a S F B&B – it'll never work. You can e-mail me on board. See you soon.

Love Gran and Max

'Huh – little does she know,' said Mum, who was reading the postcard over Frankie's shoulder. 'This place is going to be a hit.'

Dad took the postcard from Frankie. 'She seems to be having a good time,' he said.

'All right for some,' said Mum.

Frankie thought it was just as well Gran was on the cruise and couldn't see what was happening to her house. She could be a bit difficult sometimes and definitely didn't approve of the B&B. When Mum and Dad had told her about their idea she'd sighed loudly and said: 'Another of your harebrained moneylosing schemes!'

'But Mum, we really think this idea is a good one. This place could be a real success,' Dad had said.

'Like your writing's a success?' Gran had replied scornfully.

18

Poor Dad. Frankie had felt really sorry for him. He'd looked so uncomfortable. Gran was always saying that she thought he was wasting his time writing stories that no one wanted to publish. But Dad loved writing. He was never happier than when he was thinking of his next SF adventure.

'You'd be able to support your family properly if you just had a proper job. You had a good education. It wouldn't be hard to find real work,' Gran said.

Dad had looked like he was feeling a bit sick.

'You could have been a geologist, like Max.'

Everyone looked at Maximilian. Maximilian hadn't said anything. But Mum had scowled at him anyway. She didn't get on with her mother-in-law's boyfriend – even though he was always as nice as pie to her. She said she had a 'bad feeling' about him. The way she acted anyone would think he was a criminal master-mind instead of a retired geologist. Max was very handsome – in a sculptured, TV star sort of way. Perhaps that was why Mum didn't like him.

'He's just too *smooth*,' she said. 'And what do we really know about him? Where did he come from? Anyone could say they were a geologist.'

But no one listened to her.

Frankie thought Gran was old enough to choose her own boyfriend without Mum vetting him. When Grandad had died Gran had missed him terribly. For almost a whole year she wouldn't even let Frankie and her parents visit. That was why it was so good when she met Maximilian and started living again. And if she hadn't met Maximilian then she couldn't have moved in with him and they wouldn't have had Gran's house to turn into the B&B. So Frankie thought Mum should be grateful to Maximilian instead of hating him.

'I'm going down to the basement,' Frankie said, taking the postcard with her. She'd sort of adopted the basement as her den and loved it down there. OK, it was overcrowded but it was private too. She could play her music as loudly as she liked and no one could hear it. Plus it was huge, with a window at one side, large enough to climb through, leading to the garden. She'd put her computer on the bench just below it so she could look out when she was doing her homework.

Gran and Grandad, when he'd been alive, had used the basement as their laboratory and it still had a lot of scientific equipment in it. There was a medical skeleton in one corner and loads of scientific textbooks in the bookcases.

Most of the rest of the basement was used for storage. Mum and Dad had put their weird and wonderful SF collection down there. It included lifesize cardboard cutouts of the lead characters in the early *Star Wars* movies, and costumes and props from others. They even had a remote-controlled Dalek from *Doctor Who* that said, '*Exterminate, exterminate,*' in its funny voice. Some things in their collection, like the early toys and costumes from films, were worth quite a lot of money, not that they'd ever sell any.

As well as Mum and Dad's SF collection the basement had Gran's overflow in it. Things that wouldn't fit into Maximilian's flat. By one wall there were three suitcases with 'Do Not Open' labels stuck on them. Frankie didn't know why Gran didn't want anyone to look at her old clothes, which she was sure was all that was in the suitcases. Frankie hadn't looked inside them but the suitcases were the squashy kind so she'd given them a squash.

As well as the boxes and suitcases, Gran had left three trunks – two smaller grey ones and a large black one. The trunks had 'Private' labels stuck on them. Frankie was dying to see what was inside but they were padlocked and although she'd looked she couldn't find the keys.

Frankie switched on her computer and sent an e-mail to her Gran.

Internet Mail	File Edit View Insert Format Tools Help **SEND**
Inbox: 14 messages Sent Mail: 3 messages	Sender: Frankie Subject: hello gran! Time: 19.46

```
Hi Gran,
Thanks for the postcard. School isn't too bad.



```

Frankie stopped writing. What she wanted to say was: I wish I was over in the Galapagos Islands too. School's a

21

disaster and I have to produce a photo of a boyfriend I don't have by Monday morning. Help!!! But she couldn't e-mail that to Gran because she wasn't that kind of a gran. So instead she wrote:

Internet Mail	File Edit View Insert Format Tools Help **SEND**
Inbox: 14 messages Sent Mail: 3 messages	Sender: Frankie Subject: hello gran! Time: 19.46

```
Hi Gran,
Thanks for the postcard. School isn't too bad.
Glad you're having fun.
Frankie.
```

She pressed 'Send'.

It smelt a bit musty down in the basement, so Frankie decided to open the window. The rusty bolt was hard to move, but slowly she inched it back, pushing all her weight behind it. She was almost there when disaster struck. Just as she was pulling her hardest the bolt came off in her hand and she went flying. She knew she mustn't bump into her computer and swerved as she fell but then knocked into one of the bookcases that had Gran's books in it instead and the books came tumbling down on top of her.

'Oh no!' Frankie cried. 'Ouch!'

Then she saw the glint of something metallic amongst the fallen books – a key! A padlock-sized key. She'd pick the books up later. Even the boyfriend problem was temporarily forgotten. The key might fit one of the padlocked trunks!

Frankie knelt down beside one of the smaller grey trunks first and tried the key in the padlock, but it didn't fit. She turned to the next one, but no luck there either.

She sighed. Maybe the key wasn't for the trunks after all.

She wasn't feeling hopeful as she turned to the third and largest of the trunks. But this time the key did slip into the lock and with a little pressure she was able to turn it and the padlock sprang open.

Frankie held her breath as she pushed up the lid, then screamed with terror. A hand stretched out to her.

Inside the trunk was a chopped-up body!

Frankie scrambled away from the trunk as fast as she could, shaking with fear. No one came rushing down to help her – the basement was too well soundproofed for anyone to hear her scream. And anyway Dad was probably listening to 'Space Odyssey' and Mum'd be back in her studio.

After a few minutes Frankie stopped shaking. She steeled herself to take another peep at the body inside the trunk and realised there was something strange about the hand. It looked too rigid, but then didn't people go rigid after they were dead? She tried to remember all the things she knew about dead people. *Rigor mortis* meant stiff dead. But didn't dead bodies look bloody? The chopped-off hand didn't seem to have any blood attached to it. Maybe the blood had drained away, but shouldn't it have left a stain?

Frankie inched closer to the trunk to take a better look.

Maybe the blood had drained out. Frankie felt a bit sick at the thought. But shouldn't a dead body smell? Frankie sniffed. No. There was definitely no smell coming from the body in the trunk.

Had Gran been killing people and hiding them down in the basement? No, Gran couldn't. Gran a mad serial killer? No, no, no. It didn't make sense. Gran always wore suits and had tidy hair. She was much too smart to be a murderer – wasn't she?

Frankie inched closer to take another look. She'd almost reached the trunk when the hand fell out with a horrible thunk. Frankie screamed again, even louder. But she didn't run away this time. There was definitely something wrong with the hand. It had electronic-looking stuff inside the wrist. You didn't need to be a scientist to know that wasn't right.

Then Frankie realised she wasn't looking at a trunk full of *human* body parts. She was looking at a trunk full of robot body parts. Body parts of a robot that looked just like a person – an android.

Frankie was now too curious to feel scared. She knelt down beside the trunk to take a closer look.

Gran had never mentioned making a robot, but then she hardly ever spoke about the work she and Grandad used to do in their laboratory. But if Gran and Grandad had made a robot that had worked wouldn't everyone know about it – wouldn't it have been all over the TV and newspapers? So maybe it hadn't worked. Frankie pulled bits out of the trunk. The robot seemed to be all there – legs, arms, torso, feet, hands . . . And there was a computer disk in the trunk too. Frankie put it to one side to have a look at later.

The robot head was wrapped in some sort of protective bubble-wrap. It had a moist feel to it. Carefully Frankie pulled the covering away. Then stared at the robot head in amazement.

She didn't know exactly what she'd expected it to look like. Like a shop mannequin, maybe. But it wasn't plasticky at all. The head was definitely a he, and an utterly and completely gorgeous he. Not even a little bit stereotypically robot-like. It was an imagine-the-most-handsome-teenage-boy-you-can-and-then-double-it sort of head. He had great hair – black and curly – it had to be a wig, but it looked and felt like human hair. And he had great skin with a slight tan to it. And he had nice lips and a perfect nose and the longest eyelashes. Frankie gave his hair a gentle tug, to see if the wig would come off, but it must have been inserted into his head, because it didn't. She wished she could see what colour his eyes were, but his eyelids were closed. She tried pushing them up but they didn't budge. The robot teenager looked as if he was sleeping.

Frankie had stared at him for a few seconds before an

excited voice inside her head started shouting that she'd found the answer to her boyfriend problem. All she had to do by Monday was produce a photo of a boyfriend – any teenage boy would do. And it didn't have to be a full length photo. A head shot would be fine. Just one head shot . . .

Frankie smiled. 'Hello, Romeo,' she said to the robot head. 'Meet your new girlfriend. I'm Frankie.'

Frankie rushed out of the basement, raced up the stairs to her bedroom and found her camera. She took a poster of a seagull flying across a bright blue sky from one wall, a poster of a golden sunset from another and some Sellotape from a drawer.

Then she opened a cupboard and grabbed two woolly hats, two scarves and a pair of skiing goggles, found a black T-shirt for Romeo to wear and an orange swimsuit for herself. She was about to go out of the door when she saw her sunglasses on a shelf and took them too. They'd be ideal for hiding Romeo's closed eyes. The robot head was perfect in every other way. And Wendy and Leanne need never know that all she'd got was a head, not a real living boyfriend – because she could angle her camera so it only took a head shot.

Frankie felt like dancing. All her troubles were over. Her lie need never be found out and maybe she could make some real friends at school. She could have skipped down the stairs, if she wasn't carrying so much stuff.

'You OK, Frankie?' Dad called from his study.

'Yes,' she called back.

'What are you doing with those posters?'

'Um . . . er . . . I'm just decorating the basement.'

'Oh . . . good idea,' he said and went back to typing into his laptop.

Back in the basement Frankie pulled a table over to a wall and stuck the seagull poster behind it. It made the ideal background for a beach shot. She put the sunglasses on the robot's face and wrapped the black T-shirt around its neck. Then she threw off her own clothes and struggled into her swimsuit, but left her socks on because the stone floor was cold.

Once Romeo was carefully positioned on top of a box on the table Frankie ran over to the camera.

'That should do it.'

She pressed the delay button, ran back to Romeo, and rested her head against his.

'Cheese!'

She took four beach day shots. Then she took the seagull poster down and stuck the sunset poster to the wall.

She ran back to the camera, pressed the delay button, ran back to the robot. She tried to look at Romeo like a girl in love – but it wasn't easy because she wasn't sure how a girl in love should look. Sort of simpering? She tried imagining that she was looking at a cute puppy. That'd have to do.

Sunset shots done, Frankie turned the seagull poster on its side so that it would only show bright blue sky for the last lot of the photos – the skiing ones.

She pulled on her woolly hat and ski goggles.

'Frankie!' Mum called. Frankie froze, then looked down at her swimsuit and socks. Her heart began to beat at a million times a minute. Was her mum going to come downstairs? There were going to be an awful lot of awkward questions if she did.

'Supper's nearly ready.'

Phew! She wasn't coming downstairs.

'Up in a minute,' Frankie called back.

Quickly she put the other ski hat and goggles on Romeo and scarves round each of their necks. She ran over to the camera and pressed the delay button, then ran back to the robot. She kissed him on the cheek – 'Uurgh!' He wasn't very nice to kiss. His skin felt cold and lifeless.

Frankie took two more photos but just put her lips close to his face – it would still look as if she was about to kiss him, or had just finished kissing him.

'It's on the table,' Mum called.

'Coming!'

The film rewound itself.

Frankie carefully covered the robot head with its covering, put it back inside the trunk and turned the key in the padlock. She didn't want Mum or Dad to know about him yet; he was her secret, at least for now. If she told them about him they'd only want to use him as another prop for the B&B and she didn't want that. He was hers. Her hero.

And anyway she couldn't tell them about Romeo because then she'd have to say she'd opened one of Gran's locked trunks – when Gran had said very clearly that no one was to touch any of her things.

'Please let just one of the photos come out looking all right,' Frankie wished, crossing her fingers.

'Frankie!'

Frankie threw her uniform on over her swimming costume and raced up the stairs.

'You look very flushed, Frankie, I hope you're not coming down with something,' Mum said.

'I'm fine,' Frankie replied. 'What's for supper?'

The next day Frankie took the film into the PhotoExpress shop in the indoor shopping centre to be developed. For the next hour she wandered impatiently around the shopping centre, hardly seeing what was in any of the shops. Every few seconds she checked her watch. It seemed to take forever. But at last the 3600 seconds had ticked by and it was time to go back.

Frankie's hands shook as she paid for the photos and took the packet as carefully as if it were a newly laid egg. She walked out of the shop smiling and then stopped dead. Wendy and Leanne were walking straight towards her! They mustn't see the photos until she'd checked through them. Luckily, they stopped to look in a shoe shop window. They hadn't seen her yet. But if they looked round . . . Frankie dived behind the litter bins and crouched low to the ground.

A minute ticked slowly past, then another.

How long should she wait before coming out? Would they have gone past yet? The bins didn't smell too good. Her foot was on an old curry splodge, her head next to some antique grey chewing gum. But she couldn't get up until she was sure they'd gone.

'Er . . . Frankie, what are you doing down there?' a voice said.

Frankie almost died of fright.

She looked up and saw Darren's puzzled face. Thank goodness it was only him.

'I'm hiding from Wendy and Leanne,' Frankie hissed back at him. 'See if they've gone, will you?'

Darren sighed, 'OK,' and walked away.

'Can't see them anywhere,' Frankie heard him say a few seconds later.

Frankie stood up. 'Thanks.'

'Have you sorted out your boyfriend trouble?' Darren asked.

'Yes, all sorted,' said Frankie, holding out the packet of photos. 'Wendy and Leanne are going to be sick when they see these.'

'So you have got a boyfriend?' said Darren, sounding depressed.

'No,' said Frankie. 'But I found a way to make it look as if I've got one in these photos. Look, I'll show you.'

She opened the packet and was just about to show Darren the photos when his dad walked up. Poor Darren spent most of his time trying to pretend his dad wasn't a teacher at Brentfield. But no one would let him forget it.

'Hello, Frankie,' Mr Quayle said. He was very tall and usually serious. Frankie found him a bit intimidating. Even when he was smiling at her, as he was now.

'Oh hi, Mr Quayle.'

Frankie didn't want Mr Quayle to see the precious photos. She put them behind her back.

'I've been thinking of starting an after-school science club, Frankie, would you be interested in joining?' he asked.

'Yes,' Frankie said.

'Good. We need more people like you – students who really enjoy science. I might even enter us for the School Science Club of the Year quiz.'

'I'm going to be in the Science Club too,' Darren told Frankie.

Mr Quayle looked surprised. 'I thought you said you'd have to think about it.'

'I have thought about it and I do want to be in it,' Darren said.

Frankie really wanted to go home and look at the photos.

'Well, I'd better be going. See you on Monday,' she said, backing away a few steps. Then she turned and hurried off.

Maybe it was just as well she hadn't told Darren about the robot head. She thought she could trust him, but she hadn't known him very long. She decided to keep quiet about it for the moment.

When Frankie got home she took the photos down to the basement. The first one she looked at was the one where she'd tried to look like a girl in love. It was awful . . . She looked like she was drunk.

But the one where she'd kissed the robot's clammy skin was good. And the very first beach shot she'd taken was the best of all.

She came out of the basement, whistling.

'You sound happy,' Dad said.

'I am,' said Frankie. 'How's the book going?'

'Great,' Dad said. 'I really think this one's got a good chance of being published.'

Wendy and Leanne were waiting for Frankie when she walked into class on Monday morning.

'Yeah, and?' said Leanne challengingly, not looking away from her reflection as she tried out Wendy's new lipgloss.

'Where is it?' said Wendy, snatching her lipgloss back.

'Where's what?' Frankie asked, trying to act cool, even though her stomach was tying itself in knots. She sauntered over to her desk and plonked her bag on top of it.

Harriet, at the next desk, gave a sort of half smile and half smirk.

Frankie didn't know which it was. Being friendly? Harriet hadn't exactly been friendly so far. At least not on the hockey pitch, where she'd been as lethal as a space monster from Kookie. Or laughing at her? Frankie decided it was safest not to respond.

'We want to see the photo of course. The photo of *Romeo* that you promised,' Leanne said.

'To prove that he really exists,' said Wendy.

'Oh that,' Frankie said. She hoped her carefree act had fooled them. She flipped open her bag and took the photo out.

Leanne's perfectly shaped lilac-polished fingernails snatched it from Frankie.

There was silence for a few seconds. Frankie held her breath. She could hear her heart beat.

'But he looks OK,' Leanne said.

'It doesn't look like a fake,' Wendy said, sounding disappointed.

Harriet was doing her muscular combination smirk and smile again.

'It isn't,' Frankie said.

'I bet he's got lovely eyes,' sighed Wendy.

'Yes he does.'

'Shame he's wearing sunglasses.'

'What colour are his eyes?'

Frankie picked a colour.

'Er . . . blue.'

'Tell us how . . .' started Leanne, but Mr Marks, the form teacher, came in. Frankie grabbed the photo and stuck it back in her bag.

Mr Marks was the boys' PE teacher as well as Frankie's form teacher. He was short and stocky as a bulldog.

'Seats, people!' Mr Marks said.

Everyone went back to their own seats and Mr Marks barked his way through the register.

Leanne and Wendy didn't get a chance to ask Frankie more about the photo for the rest of the morning. And Frankie did her best to avoid them. She ate her lunchtime sandwiches in the furthest corner of the playground. Around her other kids from other years talked and messed about. She wished she had a friend to talk to.

'Can I see the photo of your boyfriend?' a voice asked. It was Meera, the girl who'd managed to get out of playing hockey by pretending she needed the loo.

'Sure,' Frankie said.

Meera looked closely at the now slightly bent picture, her long black hair trailing over it.

'Ooh . . . he's so cute,' she said.

'Mmm,' Frankie agreed. It felt bad lying to Meera but she didn't know her well enough to tell her the truth.

The next minute Wendy and Leanne came over and took the photo off Meera for another look.

Frankie just smiled at them. Her aim for the day, and so far she'd succeeded, was to stay cool around Wendy and Leanne.

'He doesn't look like your type,' said Leanne, as she studied the photo intently.

'So what type do you think I should have?' Frankie said.

'Someone – less cute, more normal.'

'Is he *really* your boyfriend?' Wendy asked.

'Yes!'

'Then you'll be bringing him to the school disco next month,' Leanne said, and she nudged Wendy.

'Ooh yes. Bring him to the disco, Frankie,' said Meera.

Darren walked past and Meera smiled at him but he didn't notice.

'Well . . . I'll have to ask Romeo,' Frankie said, knowing that a robot head, even if it could've talked, would have said no – because only having a head and no body would make it difficult to dance.

'A boyfriend who loved you would come to the disco, if you asked him,' Leanne said.

'He does love you, doesn't he, Frankie?' asked Wendy.

'Of course.'

'Then make sure he comes,' said Leanne.

'Because if we don't meet him then we'll think this isn't really a photo of your boyfriend . . .'

'. . . Romeo.'

'We'll think it's a photo of someone you persuaded to have his picture taken with you.'

'So you could *pretend* he was your boyfriend.'

'And that'd make you a really big liar.'

'And no one wants to be friends with a liar.'

'He *is* my boyfriend,' Frankie insisted.

'Then bring him to the disco.'

'I will!'

Oops.

4

Darren was waiting for Frankie at the school gates.

'I thought you said you didn't have a boyfriend,' he said, as they started to walk home together. He sounded cross.

'I don't.'

'Then how come just about everyone at school has seen his photo?'

'It's not what you think,' Frankie tried to interrupt, but Darren was on a roll.

'And how come you told Leanne and Wendy you'd bring him to the disco?'

'Listen Darren, I don't have a boyfriend.'

'But you've got a photo of one.'

'Yes.'

'Can I see it?'

Frankie sighed and pulled the photo of Romeo from her bag. It was getting crumpled round the edges from all the hands that had been holding it.

Darren took the photo and stared at it gloomily.

'He's really good-looking,' he sighed. 'Any girl would want to go out with *him*.'

'I'm not going out with him,' Frankie said. Why wouldn't he listen to her? 'And he isn't my boyfriend.'

'Then why did you tell Leanne and Wendy you'd bring him to the disco?'

'I don't know. It just slipped out,' Frankie said. She really wished it hadn't. If only she'd kept her big mouth shut. Part of the reason, she knew, was that Meera had been there and she wanted Meera to like her and part of it had been that she really would have liked to have had a boyfriend to go to the disco with. But neither of those reasons was good enough for getting herself in such a mess.

'I don't understand,' Darren said.

Frankie couldn't keep her secret to herself any longer. She had to tell someone or she'd burst. 'I found a way to pretend I had a boyfriend. Look, can you come round to my house?'

'Now?'

'Yes.'

'Why?'

'I've got something to show you.'

'OK.'

Darren saw the spaceship on the roof as soon as they turned down Frankie's street.

'Hey, look at that!' he said.

'Mmm,' said Frankie. He didn't know that the spaceship was on top of *her* house.

'Who'd want to have a spaceship on their roof?' Darren said.

Then he saw the aliens.

'Hey, look at those. They're excellent.'

They'd almost reached the house when Darren saw the sign in the window. 'Science fiction B&B. I've never heard of one of those before.'

'No,' Frankie agreed, as she pushed open the gate. 'Let's just hope we get lots of customers.'

'You mean you live *here*?' Darren said, as he followed her up the path.

Frankie rang the doorbell. It played the theme tune to *Men in Black*. Then she realised the door wasn't fully closed and pushed it open.

Inside a hologram of the galaxy moved around the large hallway in a slow dance. Darren's mouth fell open. He saw Frankie looking at him and shut it quickly.

'Hi Frankie,' Dad called. He was working on the light system in the corner. 'How d'you like my galaxy hologram?'

'I think the guests will love it,' Frankie said. Dad was always saying SF fans were some of the most imaginative and fun people he knew.

'This is Darren,' Frankie said.

'Hi Darren,' said Dad.

'Hi,' said Mum, coming out of the kitchen. 'What d'you think?'

'Totally amazing,' Darren said enthusiastically.

'Frankie never told me she lived in a great place like this.'

'That's because she's not always sure if it is such a great place,' Dad joked.

'Want to have a look round?' Mum asked.

'Yes,' Darren said, and before Frankie could stop them Mum and Dad were taking him on a tour of the B&B, and showing him the bedrooms that had been decorated after different SF TV series.

'This is the Babylon 5 room,' Mum told Darren, opening one door.

'And this is Deep Space 9,' said Dad, opening another.

'You're so lucky to live here, Frankie,' Darren kept saying, as she followed them from room to room, wishing the tour would be over so she could show him the *really* interesting thing she had in the basement.

'Now, how about a cup of tea in the Red Dwarf lounge?' Mum said. 'And you can tell us a bit about yourself, Darren.'

Frankie couldn't stand it any longer. 'Not now, Mum. We've got work to do.'

'Have we?' Darren said.

'Yes,' said Frankie. 'Remember the, er, project-I-was-going-to-show-you?'

Darren looked confused for a moment. Then light dawned.

'Oh – oh yes.'

'Come on Darren.'

They headed towards the basement.

'Might have a surprise for you when you come back,' Dad called after them.

'A surprise?' Darren said. 'D'you know what it is?'

'No,' Frankie shrugged, as she closed the basement door behind them. 'You never know what's going to happen next around here.' She took the key from its hiding place and went over to the trunk with the robot body parts inside it. 'Promise you'll never tell anyone what I'm going to show you.'

'But I . . .'

'Promise.'

'OK, I promise.'

'It'll be a secret – just between the two of us.'

'Right.'

'Say it.'

'It'll be a secret – just between the two of us.'

Frankie knelt beside the trunk and unlocked the padlock. 'You know I told you I'd found a way to pretend I'd got a boyfriend?'

'Yes.'

Frankie lifted the lid. 'This is how I did it.'

Darren looked into the trunk, gulped, then just stared, gobsmacked.

'How . . . what . . . is it?'

'I thought it was a murdered body when I first saw it. But it isn't. It's a dismantled robot – an android,'

Frankie told him. She unwrapped the bubble-wrap from the robot's head.

Darren was still in shock. 'The head – that's the head in your photo?' Frankie nodded. 'It's – it's so lifelike. Is it a prop from a film?'

'I don't think so. It doesn't belong to Mum and Dad. I found it in one of Gran's trucks and she hates SF movies. She says they belittle real science.'

Darren touched the robot's face. 'Its skin feels almost human.'

'Yes, although it wasn't nice to kiss. Not nice at all,' Frankie said, shuddering at the memory.

'You've been kissing it!' Darren said, looking slightly sick at the thought. 'Why?'

'For the photos, of course.'

'Oh.'

Frankie wondered why else Darren thought she'd want to kiss a dismantled robot.

She went over to the computer and clicked the mouse. The information from Gran's computer disk came up on the screen. 'And this tells us how to make it. Actually I tried reading it over the weekend. It's really confusing. We might need to ask your mum or dad to explain some of the equations – without telling them what they're for, of course.'

'But we're not going to *make* it?'

'Er no, course not, I meant if we were – just as an experiment – you know – to see if we could.' Frankie pressed 'copy'.

Darren still looked doubtful. 'Have you told your mum and dad about it?'

'No, I want to keep it a secret, at least for the time being,' Frankie said. 'Anyway, if they knew about it they'd only want to use it as a prop in the B&B.' She slipped in a blank disk and clicked 'copy' again.

'Won't your gran be cross with you for opening her trunk?' Darren said. 'It's got "Private" stuck on it.'

'Furious,' said Frankie. 'But she's still in the Galapagos Islands. What the eye doesn't see the heart doesn't grieve over, or something like that.' She'd worry about Gran later. Anyway, maybe Gran need never know that she'd found her robot.

'Copy completed' came up on the screen.

Darren looked in the trunk.

'I suppose we could check that all the parts are here. You know, just to see . . .'

Frankie grabbed a piece of paper and scribbled down a list of body parts.

'Two feet?'

'Check.'

'Ankle to knee?'

'Check.'

'Knee bits?'

'Yep. What's that?'

Frankie pulled something blue from the trunk and shook it out. It was a pair of overalls.

'His clothes?' said Darren.

44

'Must be,' said Frankie, reaching into the trunk and pulling out a thumb.

They carried on until they'd taken all the identifiable parts out, but there were still lots of strange-looking bits left, along with some tools for assembling the robot.

Darren picked up a big toe and a foot. 'I'll just see how these fit together,' he said.

'Wait!' Frankie said.

'Why?' said Darren.

'Make sure that's the correct toe for that foot. It might not be so easy to remove once you've stuck it in.'

'Great, OK.' He studied the toe. 'It's hard to tell.' He pulled off his shoes and socks and compared the robot's big toe to his own.

'Phew, Darren. Talk about cheese,' Frankie complained.

But Darren only grinned.

Frankie looked at the remaining bits in the trunk.

'It's the right big toe,' Darren said. He picked up the foot. 'And this is the right foot.'

Darren pressed the toe into the empty toe socket. There was a tiny whirring sound. Suddenly Darren dropped the foot.

'Careful!' Frankie said. She didn't want him to break the robot by being clumsy. Gran would go nuts. Darren had gone very pale. 'Are you OK, Darren?'

'Look at it,' Darren whispered, his eyes fixed on the robot foot.

Frankie picked it up. 'What?' Then she saw what Darren had seen. Where the toe now joined the foot there was no mark, not even a tiny seam, nothing to show that the toe and foot had ever been apart.

'Terminator or what,' Frankie said. She touched the toe. It looked just like a human one.

'I think it's time I went home,' Darren said. 'This is too much to handle for one night.'

Frankie put the foot down. She went over to the computer disk, took the disk out and gave it to Darren. 'I made a copy, a little bedtime reading for you, you know, just in case you were interested.'

They put all the robot bits back in the trunk and padlocked it.

As they came back into the hallway they heard the eerie call of Chewbacca, the immense ginger-brown fur-covered Wookiee warrior who was Hans Solo's co-pilot in the early *Star Wars* movies.

For a second Darren looked absolutely terrified. Then Dad came out from behind the sofa, wearing the Chewbacca costume.

'Good, eh?' he said. 'I think I got the voice just right.'

'Very good, Dad,' said Frankie.

Darren shook his head in amazement. 'I wish I lived here,' he said.

'We'll let you know if we need any Saturday staff,' Mum joked.

'Would you?' Darren said, taking her seriously and sounding as though Mum had offered him a job at Buckingham Palace. 'Really?'

'Yes,' said Dad.

'What a nice boy,' Mum said, when Darren had gone. 'Beautiful manners. He'll make someone a lovely boyfriend.' She looked at Frankie and raised an eyebrow.

'Not me!' Frankie said, horrified at the thought. 'He's just a friend, Mum. A friend who's helping me with a project.'

'Friends can become boyfriends,' Mum said.

'Not Darren,' Frankie told her mum firmly. How could her mum even think she'd want to go out with Darren? She didn't. She couldn't. Not in a million years.

'Frankie,' Darren hissed from behind a tree.

'Yes?' Frankie said, going to join him, but not sure why he wanted them to act like spies in an old movie.

'I've been thinking.'

'Yes?'

'And I've been looking at that computer disk you gave me and I think, if you want to, that we should have a go.'

'Have a go at what?'

'Have a go at making the robot.'

'Oh!'

'Ooo-ooh! Frankie's got a new boyfriend,' Wendy shouted across the playground.

Frankie ignored her but Darren looked as if he wanted to die of embarrassment.

'Come round after Science Club and we'll start,' Frankie told him.

The bell rang and Frankie hurried off to PE.

'Today we're going to pick the ten girls who are

going to be in the cheerleading squad for the school basketball team,' Miss Myers said.

'Wendy and me should be in it, miss,' Leanne said. 'Because we used to be drum majorettes.'

'Right,' said Miss Myers. 'Outside, everyone, for a warm-up before we start.'

Frankie groaned. Miss Myers' idea of a warm-up was her idea of exhaustion. But she wanted to be a cheerleader. She'd never been one before.

Unfortunately Frankie soon found that although her brain wanted to be a cheerleader her body didn't agree. It didn't want to do a cartwheel like the other girls and she toppled over instead. And it refused to do the splits either. Frankie was deselected in the first ten minutes and sat on the bench to watch until the final ten girls and one reserve were chosen.

Horrid Wendy and Leanne were picked but so were nice Harriet and Meera. Not only could Meera do great cartwheels but she could do back flips too.

'I suppose you'll be going along to the Science Club,' Leanne sneered at the end of school.

'I'd rather be in the Science Club than be a stupid cheerleader, waving pom poms about,' Frankie said. But it wasn't true. She'd have liked to have done both.

Six people went to the first meeting of the Science Club. They were Frankie, Darren, Harriet and three boys from the year below.

'I didn't know you were interested in science,' Frankie said to Harriet.

Harriet just shrugged.

Frankie smiled at her. A shrug from Harriet was a lot better than having her racing down the hockey pitch, stick in hand, towards her.

'Welcome, welcome to our first meeting of the Science Club. I have some good news already. Our school has been chosen as one of this year's Science Club of the Year entrants,' Mr Quayle said.

'But we're not a proper club yet,' said one of the boys from the year below. 'We haven't even had our first meeting.'

Mr Quayle looked embarrassed. 'Well, I did enter us before I actually knew if anyone would turn up. But I was sure *somebody* would and if I didn't enter us we'd have missed the closing date for this year and have to wait until next year to take part.'

'Will this Science Club of the Year thing be on the telly?' Harriet asked.

It was the most Frankie had ever heard her say.

'Er – yes. I think so. That hasn't been finalised yet,' Mr Quayle said.

'Probably won't be then.'

'So what do we get if we win?' asked one of the boys.

'A cup and £500.'

'£500!' Everyone now looked very enthusiastic. The whole school would have joined the Science Club if they'd known that they might get £500 for being in it. 'Each?'

'No – it's, er, £500 to spend on science equipment for your school,' Mr Quayle said, shuffling papers.

'So that's why you wanted us to enter.'

'Well, let's get on. I thought we'd look at a different area of science each week. Anyone have any requests?'

Frankie put up her hand. 'How about robotics?' she said, and winked at Darren.

Over the next two weeks Darren and Frankie spent every evening after school and all day at the weekends, building the robot down in the basement.

The Science Club gave them the perfect opportunity to ask Mr Quayle about any problems they got stuck on.

'Why are you asking me all these questions about robots?' he asked one day and Frankie felt her heart sink. Darren just opened and closed his mouth like a goldfish. Then Frankie had a brainwave.

'We're just interested because of that TV programme,' she said.

'Yeah,' said Darren, automatically agreeing with her.

'*Kookie the Space Warrior* – it's about a robot girl who fights the bad guys in space,' Frankie said.

'Oh I know the one you mean,' Mr Quayle said. 'You watch that all the time, don't you, Darren?'

'Er well – some of the time,' said Darren.

'He's got pictures of her all over his bedroom walls,' Mr Quayle told the rest of the Science Club.

Darren looked as though he wished he could sink

51

into the floor. But Mr Quayle hadn't finished yet. 'What did you say about her? Oh yes – she's hot!'

Darren couldn't take any more. 'I have to get a drink of water,' he said and dashed out of the room.

Making a robot wasn't easy, not easy at all, even for two science buffs. It was hard enough just trying to understand the computer disk Frankie had found in the trunk. Then they had to work out which part went where. The limbs were easy to figure out but there were all sorts of other things that needed to go inside the robot to make it as human and lifelike as possible. Like a body temperature regulator so the robot's skin could become warm like a human's. Unlike when Frankie kissed it. And a power management pack based on an advanced sort of lithium ion battery.

The 'brain' was the most complicated part. The computer disk showed that the robot was designed to carry on learning once it was up and running. It was programmed with something called Accelerated Intelligence.

'It's like that dog,' Darren said.

'What dog?' said Frankie.

'That robot dog they made – Aibo – it means companion in Japanese. It learns from interacting with its owner. Just like our robot will learn from interacting with people.' Darren frowned as he tried to remember what he had read. 'Oh yes – you need to keep playing and talking to it or it won't develop properly.'

'Sounds like a real dog,' Frankie said.

'Yeah, but it isn't. It has emotions but it runs on lithium ion batteries and it doesn't need to eat or sleep or go for walkies past lamp posts like a proper dog – and it doesn't bite.'

'Does it look like a dog? Does it have fur?'

'No, it looks like a robot. It can move about independently but not like a real dog. It moves like a robot.'

'Our robot looks like a real boy,' Frankie said. 'I wonder if he'll move like a real boy too – if we ever get him working.'

'He might – he's so amazing.' Darren inserted the microchip controlling the robot's face and eye movements. Romeo was complete. 'Watch this,' he said.

The robot's eyelids opened to reveal bright blue eyes. Its lips twitched and it smiled a slow and sinister smile.

Frankie screamed like a banshee.

'It's OK, it's OK,' Darren said. 'Don't frighten it.'

'Me frighten *it*!' Frankie squeaked. *She* was the one who'd screamed.

'Yes, but remember he's a bit like that dog, Aibo, only a lot more advanced. So if you shout at him you'll hurt his feelings and if you scream at him he'll be frightened.'

Frankie looked over at Romeo. He did look scared. He was sort of cowering away from her.

'So what am I supposed to do?' she hissed at Darren.

'Just try being friendly.'

'OK,' said Frankie. 'Hi,' she smiled at the robot. 'I'm Frankie.'

'Frankie,' the robot repeated.

'And this is Darren.'

'Hi,' said Darren, giving a little wave.

'Hi, Darren,' said the robot carefully. Then he raised his arm and imitated Darren's wave.

'And you're Romeo,' Frankie said, pointing at him.

'I'm Romeo,' said the robot, pointing to himself.

'That's it,' said Frankie and she smiled.

Romeo tried to copy the smile. Smiling wasn't easy for him. He had to try a few different movements of his face before he got the hang of it. But he got it right in the end. Frankie and Darren laughed and after a second of watching them Romeo joined in with a totally unnatural-sounding laugh noise.

'He'll need some shoes,' Frankie said. There'd only been the overalls in the trunk and the basement floor was not only cold, which wouldn't affect the robot, but uneven and rough too, which might.

Darren looked down at his own feet. They were big for a boy of his height. He was about ten centimetres shorter than Romeo. Then he looked over at Romeo's feet. 'He looks about my size,' he said. He unzipped his bag. 'I've got these.' He pulled out a very old pair of trainers that smelt of feet. 'I've been using them for PE, but Mum said she's going to get me some new ones at the weekend.'

'Right,' Frankie said, 'you put them on him.' She

wanted to keep as far away from Darren's smelly old trainers as possible.

'They're not *that* bad,' Darren said. He pushed the trainers onto Romeo's feet and did up the laces.

Frankie didn't say anything. Darren obviously had a foot problem.

'Frankie, we're just popping out to get some fish and chips,' Mum called from upstairs.

'OK,' Frankie called back.

'You staying for supper, Darren?' Mum called.

'Yes please.'

Darren was round their place so often now it was like he'd moved in. Not that one more person moving in would have made much difference to Mum or Dad. The B&B regularly had strangers wandering around it these days. Frankie was glad she'd got a lock for the basement. It'd be bad enough if Mum or Dad found the robot, and she certainly didn't want one of the guests discovering him. Fortunately her mum and dad had been too busy to pay much attention to what Frankie and Darren were doing.

The only real problem had come when Mum and Dad had wanted to turn the basement into an alien planet complete with all their alien creature props as well as the Daleks and C3PO and R2D2 from *Star Wars* – robots that looked more like robots than people. But Frankie had begged and sulked and made a huge fuss until they'd backed down and decided to put the alien lounge in the attic instead.

Frankie and Darren had volunteered to be removal men and taken all the SF props up from the basement.

Romeo learned faster than any human could have done but there was so much to teach him that at times Frankie almost wished they hadn't made him at all. It wasn't just the letters and numbers and writing, which he grasped with ease, but all the other social things that any teenage boy would have learnt naturally over the years. Things he'd have just learnt from being alive. Like identifying different smells and knowing basic safety – like don't talk to strangers and never get into a stranger's car. There was almost too much for him to learn. It was lucky he was programmed with accelerated intelligence so that he could continue learning by himself.

Whilst Frankie was at school he spent hours on the Internet and watching TV. He stayed in the basement all the time and Frankie locked the basement door whenever she went out.

Every now and again she'd feel guilty for not telling Gran what she'd done. She was very glad that the Galapagos Islands were so far away. But Gran would have to come back some time. And Frankie didn't think she was going to be too pleased with her when she found out what she'd done.

6

One Saturday morning Frankie went downstairs to find Romeo staring out of the basement window.

'I want to go out,' he said. 'Out there.'

'OK,' Frankie said. It was time he saw what the world outside the basement was like. 'When Darren gets here we'll go into town.'

At that moment the thing that Frankie had been dreading happened. She'd forgotten to bolt the basement door and Mum opened it and walked down the stairs.

'Hi Frankie, we're just popping out to get some paint,' Mum said. Then she saw Romeo. 'Oh hello, I didn't realise Frankie had a friend round. Are you working on the same project as Frankie and Darren?'

'I am the project,' Romeo said.

Mum looked a bit confused. 'Er, right – OK. Frankie, we won't be long.'

As soon as Mum had gone Frankie said, 'Remember you must never tell anyone you're a robot.'

'Must never tell anyone I'm a robot,' Romeo repeated. 'Rule number one.' He grinned and Frankie grinned back at him.

A few minutes later Darren tapped on the basement window and Frankie let him in.

'We're going out,' Romeo told him.

Darren raised an eyebrow at Frankie. 'All of us?'

Frankie nodded. 'I think we can risk a walk outside,' she said.

'Great,' said Darren. He looked down at Romeo's bare feet. 'Where are your shoes?'

Romeo didn't usually bother to wear Darren's shoes and Frankie had got tired of having to tell him to put them on all the time. The basement floor didn't seem to be doing any damage to whatever the soles of his feet were made of. But he'd have to put the trainers on to go outside.

'I don't want to wear them,' Romeo complained. 'They smell funny.'

'They don't smell that bad,' Darren said.

Frankie secretly thought that they did. But she looked for them anyway.

The ancient trainers were hidden behind one of the smaller trunks. She picked them up by the laces and held them out to Romeo.

Romeo shook his head. 'I don't want to wear those smelly shoes.'

Darren and Frankie tried and tried to persuade him to put them on but Romeo wouldn't.

'Please put the trainers on Romeo – for me,' Frankie said.

'Nope.' Romeo shook his head and did a sort of pout. He looked very cute when he sulked, but Frankie wasn't going to tell him that.

'Stop messing about. Put these shoes on now!' she said firmly.

'No, no, no!' Romeo said, and stamped his feet. He grabbed the trainers and threw them across the basement.

'We won't be able to go out if you keep behaving like this.'

'I don't care!' he shouted. But Frankie knew that he did really. She'd seen the way he'd been looking longingly out of the basement window.

'I'll see if I can find you some other shoes to wear,' she said, and crept up the stairs and into Mum and Dad's room. Mum and Dad were back with the paint and working on the alien lounge in the attic above her.

Frankie opened Dad's closet and looked inside. Only two pairs of shoes! He was sure to notice if she took one of them. Then she spotted a pair of Mum's old red flip-flops at the back of the closet. They'd have to do. Frankie took them downstairs.

'Here you are Romeo, lovely red shoes.'

Romeo's face lit up with delight. He needed no persuading to put them on.

'I like these shoes, Frankie. They don't smell.'

As Romeo walked through the front gate and looked out at the ordinary street, he started to shake with fear.

'What's the matter?' Frankie asked.

'The world's so big. I'm scared. Hold my hand, Darren.'

Darren took Romeo's hand. Romeo stopped shaking.

'You'd better take Romeo's other hand, Frankie,' Darren said.

'Why?' Frankie asked.

'Because you're his girlfriend,' Darren said.

'Aren't you my girlfriend, Darren?' Romeo asked.

'No, I'm a boy. You can let go of my hand now.'

'No, I like holding it.'

Darren shrugged. 'I hope I don't bump into anyone I know,' he said.

'Butchers . . .' Romeo said, as they walked past the first of the shops.

'And I hope I don't bump into anyone I know,' Frankie said.

'Newsagents . . . cake shop . . . CD shop – what's that?' Romeo asked, pointing to a large modern grey building with steps leading up to it and statues outside it.

'That's the Convention Centre. They hold lots of Science Fiction events there.'

On the noticeboard outside the Convention Centre there was a huge poster showing a very pretty girl in a leotard sort of outfit, holding a laser gun. Her picture had 'Kookie – coming soon' written underneath it.

'Who's Kookie?'

'Just someone off the telly,' Frankie told him.

'She's so beautiful,' Romeo said.

'Mmm,' Frankie said, but she wasn't really listening. She'd seen someone staring at them from across the street. She supposed they did look a bit odd, all three of them holding hands.

Or maybe it was the clothes Romeo was wearing that attracted the attention. Maybe they shouldn't have come into town. But Romeo was having a great time. His eyes were everywhere as he took in everything that he'd only ever seen on the Internet and TV and in books before.

'. . . furniture shop . . . cycle shop.'

'Oh no,' Darren said.

'What?' Frankie said, then saw what he'd seen – Wendy and Leanne!

They were walking just in front. They'd have bumped into them in another minute. Luckily Wendy and Leanne hadn't seen them yet, but they would if one of them looked round.

'. . . odd stuff shop.'

'Quick – in here,' Darren said, and he pulled Romeo and Frankie into an Oxfam shop.

'Hello,' Romeo said to the lady behind the counter. 'You've got lots of lovely things in your shop.'

'Thank you,' she smiled. 'Every time you buy something it helps somebody in need.'

'Then I'd like to buy everything.'

'They've gone,' Darren said to Frankie.

'Come on Romeo,' Frankie said. 'Time to go home.'

'But I want to buy this,' Romeo said, holding up a straw hat. 'To help people in need.'

'How much?' Frankie asked.

'Just have it,' the lady said.

'Thank you,' Romeo said, and put the hat on as they left the shop. 'Do I look handsome, Frankie?' he asked.

Frankie tried not to laugh. 'Yes, you look very handsome,' she said

Romeo kept stopping to admire his reflection in shop windows all the way down the street.

As they approached Frankie's house they saw smoke drifting up from a building site.

'What's that, Frankie?' Romeo asked.

'It's the smoke from a bonfire.'

'Like in my book. I've never seen a real bonfire.'

The next second Romeo had let go of Frankie and Darren's hands and was running towards the fire.

'I want to touch it!' he cried.

'Hey you!'

'You can't come in here!' shouted the builders.

'Stop!' Frankie screamed.

Romeo stopped just before his fingers touched the fire. He looked back at Frankie. He looked upset.

Frankie ran over to him.

'What's wrong, Frankie? Why are you shouting at me?'

'The bonfire's dangerous,' Frankie gasped. 'You

mustn't touch it. It'll burn you and that will hurt –
lots.'

'Bonfires are bad?'

'Only if a person gets too close,' Darren said, coming
to join them. 'Look.' He took Romeo's hat off and
threw it into the bonfire.

Romeo stared transfixed as it burned.

'That's what happens to a person when they touch
the fire,' Darren said.

'They go up in flames?'

Darren nodded.

'They die?'

'They could die. If they were trapped by the fire and
no one came to rescue them.'

'But if they were rescued they'd be OK?'

'Yes, if they were rescued quickly and the fire hadn't
burnt them.'

'And if they hadn't breathed in the smoke – that can
suffocate people,' Frankie added.

'I understand,' Romeo said.

'You kids – clear off,' the builders told them.

'Come on Romeo,' Frankie said, taking Romeo's
hand.

'OK, Frankie.'

Almost every school day either Leanne or Wendy
would say, 'Don't forget you promised to bring your
boyfriend to the disco.' 'I know, I know,' Frankie
would reply. She didn't really have any intention of

going to the disco at all. She'd decided she just wouldn't turn up and when they asked her what had happened to her she'd make some excuse, like she wasn't feeling well or they'd had a party for her dad's birthday so she couldn't come. Or even, and she thought this was a stroke of genius, that she and Romeo had split up. Then she wouldn't have to lie about having a boyfriend any more.

But gradually, as Romeo become more and more like a real teenage boy, Frankie became more and more tempted. Could she do it? Should she do it? Dare she take her robot to the school disco? He'd be the most handsome boy there by a long way. Leanne and Wendy would be sick with jealousy. But could he pass as a real boy? He'd passed when they'd gone into town. Mum had thought he was just one of Frankie's friends when she'd met him. And, it'd be dark and noisy at the disco which was good and it'd only be for a few hours which was good too.

Frankie asked Darren what he thought.

'Too risky!' he said. 'Look, if you want someone to go to the disco with you I – I'll go.'

Frankie looked at Romeo's handsome face. 'But you're not Romeo,' she said, and didn't see how hurt Darren was.

'You're my boyfriend, Romeo,' she told him.

Romeo frowned. 'Boyfriend – like on TV?'

'That's it. Like on the TV,' Frankie said. 'And you're coming to the school disco with me and you have to be really good, pretend you're my boyfriend and don't tell anyone that you're a robot.'

'A disco is like a party, right?' Romeo asked.

'Yes,' Frankie said.

Romeo beamed. One of his favourite books was about a party.

'I don't like it,' Darren said. 'It's too risky. What if someone realises he's a robot?'

Frankie shook her head. No one was going to think that. 'Look, there's a lot of things people might think – he's weird, he's stupid, maybe even that he's mad. But no one, absolutely no one, is going to truly believe that he is a robot who looks exactly like a boy, are they? I mean it's just not something that happens, is it? There just aren't robots that look like people walking about in the real world, are there?'

'No,' Darren said. 'But I still don't like it.'

'But you'll help us anyway?'

'Yes, I'll help you. Don't I always?'

'You're a good mate, Darren.'

'I know I am.'

'Right, the first thing we need are some clothes for Romeo to wear to the disco. He can't go in those overalls and red flip-flops.'

'I don't know if my clothes'll fit him,' Darren said doubtfully. 'They might be a bit small.'

'They will be,' Frankie said. 'And my dad's clothes'll be too big.'

'Yeah, he looks like he's about Terry's size.'

'Perfect!' said Frankie.

Terry was Darren's older brother.

'What d'you mean perfect? Terry'll kill me if he thinks I've been touching any of his clothes. He'll never agree to let me lend them to Romeo.'

Frankie sighed. Darren would never make a master criminal.

'But he won't know, will he?' she said slowly.

'Huh?'

'You'll just borrow them when he isn't looking and put them back the same way. He won't even know they've been gone.'

'But . . .'

'Trust me, it'll be fine.'

'I don't think . . .'

'It will.'

'All right,' Darren said grudgingly.

On the evening before the disco he borrowed a white T-shirt and some jeans from his older brother. He also brought round his newest pair of trainers for Romeo – they were too new to smell of anything but plastic.

'New clothes and shoes,' Romeo said enthusiastically, 'I like these.'

Quick as a flash he'd taken the overalls off and put on his new clothes, courtesy of Terry and Darren.

The transformation was amazing. Romeo looked really cool.

'Wow,' Frankie said. Wendy and Leanne were going

to be totally sick with jealousy when they saw him.
'Wow.'

Darren scowled. 'Looks OK I suppose,' he said,
which was the understatement of the year.

'What are you like at dancing, Darren?' Frankie
said.

'Hopeless.'

'Hmm. I'm not much good either.'

'What's dancing, Frankie?' asked Romeo.

'Something you do at a disco.'

Frankie switched on her CD player.

'Come on, Darren,' Frankie said. 'Let's show him
what you do.'

Darren started dancing awkwardly out of step, his
arms waving stiffly like a scarecrow. Frankie felt really
self-conscious at first. But gradually they relaxed and
got into it a bit more. Romeo loved it.

'Can I try, can I try, Frankie?' he said, jumping off his
chair.

'Not yet. Sit down and watch for a few more minutes,' Frankie said, as a slow dance came on. 'This is
how you dance when the music slows down.'

She put her arms around Darren's shoulders.

'Why's Darren's face gone pink?' Romeo asked.

'Because he's embarrassed,' Darren said, through
gritted teeth.

'Should I be embarrassed when I dance with you,
Frankie?'

'No.'

The slow dance music ended and a faster tune came on.

Romeo jumped up and copied Darren and Frankie, a look of pure happiness on his face.

'This is so much fun, Frankie,' he said and he spun round and round. It seemed as if he'd never tire. But Frankie and Darren did. After three songs they sat down and watched Romeo. He danced on and on and just got better and better.

'Remember, you have to be very sensible and grown-up tonight,' Frankie told Romeo, as they walked through the school gates the next evening.

'You can trust me, Frankie,' Romeo replied.

Miss Myers was on guard duty at the hall door. She looked pretty in a short yellow dress and long silver earrings with daisies on the end.

'Two dates, Frankie? You are popular,' Miss Myers said, when she saw Darren and Romeo.

Frankie gave the three tickets to Miss Myers and pushed open the hall door. Inside streamers swayed from the walls and balloons floated from the ceilings. Coloured lights danced around the room, shining on a smiling face here, a fast-moving body there. The music was deafening. Romeo put his fingers in his ears.

'Too loud!' he shouted at Frankie.

'That's what it's like at discos,' Frankie shouted back.

'I'm going to take my ears off and turn down the sound in my head,' Romeo said.

'No!' Frankie shouted. 'Leave your ears alone.'
Romeo taking his ears off was the last thing she
needed. It would ruin everything.

Around them some of the pupils and teachers and a
few of the parents, who'd volunteered to be chaper-
ones, were shouting and miming at each other too. But
everyone else was busy dancing.

Meera came over. She had on jeans and a cut-off lilac
T-shirt.

'Hi Meera,' Frankie said.

'Hi,' said Meera.

'This is Romeo.'

'Oh right, hi Romeo,' Meera said.

'Hi,' said Romeo, and he grinned.

But Meera only had eyes for Darren.

'Hello Darren,' she said, and took hold of his hand.
Darren looked down at his hand in hers, then back up
to her face.

'Oh . . . er hi,' he said.

Meera pulled him towards the centre of the hall.
'Let's dance.'

Darren looked over at Frankie. 'But . . .'

'Go on,' Frankie said, and made a go motion with
her hand.

Darren looked back at Frankie and shrugged help-
lessly as he was led away. Frankie waved him good-
bye. It felt peculiar not having him to help her with
Romeo, but she'd manage. Meera must really like
Darren. Strange. Darren was great to have as a friend,

but Frankie had never thought anyone might fancy him.

Then Frankie saw Wendy. She had on a skintight strapless pink plastic mini dress. She needed to pull the top up every now and again to stop it from escaping. Leanne had on a similar dress in gold.

When they spotted Romeo they stopped dancing and stared. Then Leanne nudged Wendy and they started to weave their way through the dancers towards them.

'Hi,' Leanne said to Romeo, ignoring Frankie.

'Hi,' Romeo said.

'I'm Wendy,' Wendy told Romeo, holding out a hand. Romeo shook it vigorously.

Frankie wondered if she'd become invisible. Neither Wendy or Leanne had bothered to say hello to her.

'I'm Romeo,' Romeo told Leanne and Wendy. 'And this is my girlfriend Frankie and over there, already dancing, is my good friend Darren.'

Wendy and Leanne were both leaning close, trying to hear Romeo above the loud music. Frankie looked over at Darren. He saw her and made a thumbs up sign and kept dancing with Meera.

Then, one of the tunes that had been on the CD player when Romeo had learnt to dance started to play.

'I know this song,' Romeo cried, and dragged Frankie towards the dance floor.

Frankie looked back at Leanne's startled and envious

face. She laughed. It was risky, it was crazy but she might as well enjoy herself.

Of course, Romeo wasn't prepared to dance out of the way at the side of the dance floor like Darren and Meera. He pushed his way to the front, taking Frankie with him.

'Here's a good place to dance,' he said, stopping just below the stage.

'Right.'

At first, Romeo danced in the way Frankie had shown him, but better – then he started to notice the other dancers around him and began to copy their moves instead. But better.

After about four dances, Frankie got hot and thirsty, but Romeo didn't.

'I'm going to get a drink,' she shouted.

'OK. I'll stay here.'

Frankie worked her way around the dancers to the drinks table.

'Coke, please.'

'Hi Frankie,' said two voices behind her.

'We've got lots of questions we want to ask you,' Wendy shouted above the music.

'Pardon?' Frankie shouted back.

'Questions.'

'Lots of questions.'

Frankie shrugged and held her hands up in a helpless gesture, pretending she couldn't hear them above the loud music. She looked over at Romeo. He looked very good dancing to the music. People who'd been dancing near him had drifted away, leaving a circle around him.

'Look at him move,' said Leanne.

'I'm looking, I'm looking,' said Wendy.

Romeo saw Frankie watching him. He came over to her, grinning.

'I love dancing,' he said.

'I know you do.'

'Will you dance with me now, Frankie?'

'OK.'

Romeo no longer danced the way Darren and Frankie had taught him. He had his own style and it was a thousand times cooler than Frankie's or Darren's would ever be. His body was so supple he looked like a professional. As Frankie tried to copy his moves and dance like him it was hard to remember that she'd made him from parts in Gran's trunk.

But then something went wrong. Romeo's movements stopped being beautiful and fluid. They became slow and jerky.

'Uh-oh,' Romeo said.

'Uh-oh? What d'you mean uh-oh?' Frankie said, grabbing his arm to steady him. 'What's wrong?'

'Power-pack-needs-charging,' Romeo told her in a voice that didn't sound like his normal voice at all.

Oh no. What was she going to do now? She had to get him out of the disco before anyone noticed that something was wrong. She kept a tight hold on Romeo's arm as she hustled him through the crowd.

'Excuse me, excuse me,' she said, as she pushed past the dancers who wouldn't get out of the way quickly enough. She stepped on someone's foot but could only shout 'sorry' as they pressed on. She didn't know how long Romeo would be able to keep moving. He could collapse at any moment. His face no longer had any expression on it and his walking was becoming more and more what you'd expect from a robot.

'Frankie,' Leanne said.

'Not now!' Frankie shouted and pushed past her.

Leanne was too gobsmacked to protest and just stood there, looking after them.

'Darren!' Frankie yelled.

He looked over and saw that something was very very wrong with Romeo. He left a bewildered Meera and followed Frankie and Romeo out of the hall.

'What's wrong with him,?' he asked, when they were out of sight round a corner.

'His power pack needs charging.'

'Don't-feel-good,' Romeo said.

Darren patted Romeo on the shoulder. 'Don't worry. You'll be OK.'

But Romeo didn't reply. He closed his eyes and made a strange whirring sound.

'He's completely shutting down!' Frankie cried.

They managed to catch him just before he hit the floor. Darren pushed open the science room door.

'In here.'

They carried him into the science room and propped him against one of the benches.

'What are we going to do now?' Frankie said.

'I'll run back to your house and get the spare power pack,' Darren said. 'You stay here with him.'

'OK – but hurry – run fast,' Frankie said. She was really worried.

'I'll be as quick as I can.'

'Quicker than that!' Frankie called after him as he left the science room.

Romeo was now so still he could have been a shop dummy. And because his body temperature regulator wasn't working any more he was cooling rapidly too.

'Hurry, Darren,' Frankie thought. 'Please hurry.'

She heard footsteps in the corridor. What if someone came in? Quickly she rolled Romeo under the science laboratory bench and crawled in beside him.

The science room door opened. Frankie held her breath. They couldn't be discovered. No one would understand.

'I'll just get that book for you,' she heard Mr Quayle say. He came into the room, opened a drawer and then closed it. He walked back over to the door. 'Here it is.' He went out, closing the door behind him.

Frankie was about to breathe a huge sigh of relief. But then she heard the jangle of keys and the click of a lock. Mr Quayle had locked them in!

Fifteen minutes later the door handle rattled up and down again and again.

'Frankie!' Darren called. 'Frankie, it's me, open the door.'

'I can't,' Frankie wailed from the other side. 'We're locked in.'

'Right, OK – I – I'll climb in through the window.'

A few seconds later Darren was standing outside the window. But it was too high for him to climb in. Instead Frankie climbed onto the counter near the window, stretched her hand out of it, and took the battery and a screwdriver from Darren's upstretched hand.

'Got it.'

She jumped off the counter, turned the screwdriver in Romeo's belly button to open up his torso, took out the old power pack and inserted the new one.

It only took a few minutes for Romeo to return to his normal self.

'Hello, Frankie,' he said. 'Can we do some more dancing?'

'Let's get out of here first,' Frankie said. They climbed onto the counter, out of the window and down onto the dustbin that Darren had positioned for them. A few seconds later they were back in the hall and acting as though nothing had happened.

'Where did you go?' Meera shouted at Darren. She had her hands on her hips and looked cross.

'Um . . . I got a bit hot. Just had to pop out for a minute,' he said.

Meera looked as though she didn't believe him.

A few seconds later the head teacher stopped the music.

'Well, this evening's almost over,' she said.

'Aaw,' said everyone.

'But it isn't quite over yet. It's time for the competition to find this evening's best dancers.'

'Dance with me again, please, Frankie,' Romeo begged. He pointed at the little gold cup the head teacher was holding. 'I want to win that.'

'OK,' Frankie agreed.

Romeo dragged her to the dance floor just as they put on some salsa music, which was his absolute favourite. It didn't matter that Frankie didn't have much of a clue what she was doing because Romeo knew enough for the two of them and all she had to do was relax and let him move her.

By the end of the dance they were the only two left on the dance floor and everyone cheered as the music came to an end. Frankie's face felt like it was burning and she knew she must be blushing. She'd never been applauded for dancing before. She'd hardly ever been applauded at all. The last time she could remember was when she was at infants school, playing a donkey in the Nativity play.

It was nice to be applauded, even though she knew that she wasn't the one who deserved it. Romeo would have made anyone dancing with him look good.

The head teacher smiled at them. 'The winner of the salsa is Frankie Jones and . . .'

'Romeo Chip,' said Romeo.

Frankie didn't know why he'd come up with Chip as a surname. Maybe it stood for microchip. He did have a lot of them inside him.

Romeo and Frankie went up on the stage and were given the little gold cup.

Then Romeo walked over to the microphone.

'My girlfriend, Frankie, and I would like to thank you for our prize. And – and,' he turned to the head teacher. 'I hope you will allow me to visit your school on Monday.'

'We'd love to see you. Are you staying with Frankie, then?' the head teacher said.

'Yes,' said Romeo.

Frankie was too stunned to say anything. Her mouth fell open. He was not visiting Brentfield on Monday! What was he talking about? She hadn't told him to say that.

Everyone was clapping and cheering again. Romeo took Frankie's arm and they left the stage.

Another salsa tune began.

'What . . .' Frankie started to say. But Wendy interrupted.

'Dance with me now, Romeo,' she said, pulling him towards her.

'OK.' Romeo handed Frankie his cup. 'Look after our cup, Frankie.'

'But . . .'

It was too late. They'd gone.

Frankie sighed. She'd sort it all out later. Romeo was definitely not coming to her school. It was just too risky!

She watched Wendy and Romeo dancing together and wondered if she'd looked as good as Wendy when she was dancing with him, and thought she probably hadn't.

The salsa tune ended and slow dance music came on. Leanne stampeded over to Wendy and Romeo and grabbed Romeo before Frankie, or an outraged-looking Wendy, could stop her.

'My turn now,' she said.

Close to them Miss Myers was entwined around the much shorter Mr Marks, a blissful smile on her face. The head teacher was dancing with the caretaker and Miss Gray, the English teacher, was dancing with Mr Hart, the drama teacher.

'Do you want to dance, Frankie?' Darren asked, coming over to her. 'Only if you want to, I don't mind if you don't, or do want to, but not with me.'

'Get on with it,' Wendy said, sighing loudly.

'Yes please, Darren,' Frankie said. They walked over to the dance floor. 'But where's Meera?'

'She said I wasn't paying her enough attention.'

'Oh.'

'That I kept looking at you all the time.'

'Well, you had to keep an eye on Romeo.'

'That I shouldn't have gone off without telling her.'

'Mmm.'

'So where is Meera?'

'She went to talk to Harriet.'

Frankie put her arms around Darren's neck. It felt natural and comfortable to be dancing with him. Frankie supposed it was because they'd spent so much time dancing together when they'd been showing Romeo how it was done. The dance was over very quickly.

Romeo came over to them.

'I don't want to dance with Leanne any more,' he said. 'She kept squeezing me.'

'It's time to go home anyway,' Frankie said, as the lights were switched on. 'The disco's over.'

Romeo was so happy he wanted to dance and sing all the way home. Every lamp post was a dance partner for him to twirl around, every wall a tightrope. And all the time he clung onto the little cup as if it was pure gold.

'Why did you tell Romeo he could start at our school on Monday?' Darren asked.

'I didn't!' Frankie said. 'And he isn't going to. One night at a disco is a lot different from being at school all day.'

'So what are you going to do with him, Frankie?'

'Do with him?'

'Yes. What about the future? Are you going to dismantle him now? Put him back in the trunk?'

'No!' Frankie cried. The idea made her feel sick. 'I couldn't dismantle him. It'd be like – like killing him.'

Romeo jumped onto a garden wall and danced along it.

'I'm H-A-P-P-Y!' he sang.

'I know what you mean, but you'll have to decide what to do with him eventually,' Darren said.

'Yes, but not yet.'

'Before your gran comes home.'

Frankie gulped. He was right. She'd almost forgotten about Gran coming home.

'Do you know when she's coming back?'

'No.' But it'd be in the next few weeks. She couldn't stay on a cruise forever.

They'd reached the corner of Darren's street.

'See you on Monday,' he said.

'Bye, Darren,' Romeo called from the wall.

'I need to talk to you seriously for a minute,' Frankie called out to Romeo.

Romeo jumped off the wall and ran back to her.

'What is it, Frankie?'

'I don't want you going to school with me on Monday morning.'

'OK.'

He ran back to the wall, which was now too narrow to dance along, so he tightrope-walked along it instead.

Frankie trundled along behind him. She was glad that at least that problem was over. Now all she had to deal with was Wendy and Leanne on Monday morning.

'Frankie!' Romeo cried, interrupting her thoughts. He was pointing towards the B&B. Two lifesized silver robots were getting out of a Mini that was parked in the drive.

'What are they?' he asked. He sounded scared.

'They're just robots. Go round to the basement window and let yourself in,' Frankie told him.

'But . . .'

'Go!'

He went.

'Hello?' Frankie said to the robots. 'Can I help you?'

'Take us to your leader,' said the larger of the two.

'Pardon?' said Frankie.

The smaller robot started giggling.

'Hi there,' Frankie's dad said, opening the door. 'Mr and Mrs Humphrey, is it?'

'That's us,' Mr Humphrey, the larger robot said. 'We've come for the Robots in Science Fiction Convention. Should be a blast.'

'We've been looking forward to it all year,' said the smaller robot, Mrs Humphrey.

'Come in,' Dad said. 'I'll show you to your room.'

'We spent ages making our costumes. They're shaped metal, you know,' Mrs Humphrey told Dad. She tapped on the larger robot, making a metallic clang.

Frankie shook her head as she followed the robots indoors. They'd be totally amazed if they knew she had a real-life robot down in the basement. And he wasn't made of metal and he didn't clang.

'What are they doing here, Frankie?' Romeo asked, as soon as she came down the stairs.

'They're going to the Robots in Science Fiction weekend at the Convention Centre,' Frankie said, and didn't notice how interested Romeo looked. Or realised that when she said robots what she really should have said was people dressed in robot costumes.

The next morning when Frankie went down to the basement she found that Romeo was missing. She couldn't believe it! Didn't he listen to anything she said any more? How many time had she told him he must never wander off? Where could he have gone? Then she remembered how interested he'd been in the people dressed as robots. That was it! Maybe he was talking to Mr and Mrs Humphrey. He seemed to have completely forgotten her instructions not to talk to strangers, but then he'd seen her contradict the rule more than once herself.

She knocked on the Humphreys' door but there was no answer. They must have set off for the SF Convention Centre already. Breakfast was only just over so they couldn't have been gone long. She ran outside to see if she could see them. Their car was gone. Dad was up a ladder, painting a window frame.

'Dad,' she called. 'Have you, er, seen my friend? He's called Romeo and he's around here quite often. He's quite tall with black hair.'

'Sounds like the boy who went off to the SF Centre with the Humphreys,' Dad called back.

'Oh right,' Frankie said, through gritted teeth. Now

Romeo was not only talking to strangers, he was going off with them too. 'I'll be back later.'

She ran off in the direction of the Centre. What if Romeo told the Humphreys he was a robot? She'd told him never to tell anyone. But he might think he was allowed to tell other robots. The Humphreys wouldn't believe him, would they? They couldn't. They'd just think he was lying, or mad. But what if he did something awful – like took off his head – to prove he wasn't lying?

Frankie ran faster.

She was breathless by the time she slipped into the Convention Centre with all the other hundreds of fans. Robots in science fiction movies and TV programmes were certainly popular. As she hunted for Romeo she saw people dressed as Vega from *Star Trek*, Kryten from *Red Dwarf*, a large man in leathers who kept saying 'I'll be back' like Arnie in *The Terminator*.

'Romeo Romeo wherefore art thou Romeo – you great nuisance,' Frankie muttered to herself. Part of her was cross but another part of her was sick with fear. What if someone realised he wasn't just some actor pretending to be a robot, he was the real thing.

'Hey, Frankie,' said a voice behind her and Frankie spun round. But it wasn't Romeo. It was only Darren.

'What are you doing here?' she said.

'I came to have a look and I'm, er, quite a big fan of Kookie.'

'Kookie!'

'Yeah, you know, Kookie the Space Warrior. The robot girl who's brave and beautiful.'

'I know who Kookie is,' Frankie said crossly. 'Have you seen Romeo anywhere? He went off with two people dressed as Metal Mickey who were staying at our place last night. They were coming here.'

No sooner had she said it than they saw him. He was standing with three Daleks and a man with a remote-control robot. 'There he is.' They pushed their way over. They were only just in time.

'I *am* a robot,' Romeo was saying in a loud voice. 'People made of blood and skin can't take their ears off but I can. Look.'

'Stop!' cried Frankie, grabbing hold of his arm before he could remove his ear.

'He's joking of course,' Darren told the leader of the Daleks. 'Ha ha.'

'There's always someone who gets carried away,' said the Dalek.

The man with the remote-controlled robot remote-controlled it away.

An announcer walked on to the stage. 'Take your seats please. It's the moment you've all been waiting for. Time to see some of the most popular robots on screen.'

Frankie didn't really want to stay and watch the robot screen stars. She had more than enough trouble with a robot who wasn't a screen star. But both Darren and Romeo had already sat down and were staring expectantly at the stage, as were most of the people around her. Frankie sighed and sat down too.

The show began with video clips of different robots – ranging from the more metal sort of robots like the Iron Giant, Metropolis Maria, Kryten and of course the loveable R2D2 and C3PO, to robots that looked like people, like the robots in *AI* and *Blade Runner*.

'She's so pretty,' Romeo cried, when Pris came on the screen.

'Hear hear,' said the fans around him.

'I wish you'd wear makeup like that, Frankie,' Romeo said, staring at Pris's over-made-up panda eyes. He was equally in favour of Seven of Nine from *Star Trek*, as was the man dressed as Captain Pickard sitting next to Frankie – who was holding a lifesized cardboard cutout of her.

'Is she a robot?' Romeo asked.

'No, she's a Borg,' Frankie told him.

'A Borg,' said Romeo, stretching the word out to make Borgs sound like the most wonderful things in the world, instead of dangerous half-organic and half-artificial lifeforms, at least according to *Star Trek* lore.

'And now the real reason you're here today. The star of the show – may I introduce to you Miss Jayne Crowley – better known to you all as Kookie the Space Warrior!'

Kookie ran out dressed in the leotard sort of thing she wore on the show. Then she did a couple of black flips and a cartwheel across the stage. For a second the audience was transfixed and then it went wild, cheering and screaming.

'I love you, Kookie,' Romeo shouted, jumping to his feet.

Frankie pulled him back down. 'Ssh,' she said.

'It's so good to be here,' said Kookie, into the microphone. 'And wonderful to know that the show has so many fans.'

The audience went wild once again.

'Kookie will be signing photos in the lobby after the show,' the announcer said, as Kookie cartwheeled off the stage. 'And of course you can learn more about the show on the Kookie web page.'

By now Frankie really wanted to go home, but both Darren and Romeo wanted Kookie to sign one of the very expensive photographs they'd bought, so she waited in line with them.

'You shouldn't have wasted your money,' she told Darren, who'd paid for both his and Romeo's photos.

'But we have to have photos of Kookie,' Romeo insisted. 'She's so beautiful.'

Frankie sighed. Around her people were getting ready for the next part of the day. The fashion show. Some of the costumes were really weird. She didn't know which show the three-headed robot was from.

'I love you, Kookie,' Romeo said, as he handed the actress the photo to be signed.

'Do you?' said Kookie, stifling a yawn. 'That's nice. Next.'

Romeo kept staring at Kookie's photo all the way home. Once Frankie even caught him kissing it.

'It's only pretend,' Frankie told him. 'She's not really a robot, she's just a girl – an actor – pretending to be a robot.'

But Romeo didn't listen. 'I'm going to stick this on the wall where I can see it all day and then I'm going to e-mail her,' he said. 'Kookie's the most beautiful girl in the world.'

Frankie sighed. She was getting very tired of hearing about Kookie.

9

Wendy and Leanne were waiting for Frankie at the school gates on Monday morning.

'Where is he?' Leanne said.

'He decided not to come with me,' Frankie said, trying to act cool. She carried on walking into school and they went with her.

'We want to know *everything* about him.'

'What school does he usually go to?'

'Where did you meet him?'

'Why isn't he with you this morning?'

Luckily Frankie didn't have to keep answering their questions because the bell went. She didn't think she'd ever been so pleased to hear the school bell before.

'Hi Frankie,' said Meera, as Frankie walked into the classroom followed by Leanne and Wendy.

Harriet did her odd combination smirk and smile and Frankie finally decided she was being friendly and smiled back.

The lesson before break was science with Mr Quayle.

'Good news, for those of you in the Science Club,' he said. 'The date for the competition is the sixteenth. It'll be a knockout sort of event. We're up against Hatfield first. If we win against them then we're through to the semi-finals. Oh – and it's going to be televised. The whole competition will take place on the same day but I expect they'll put it out on the TV in segments.'

Leanne put her hand up. 'Can me and Wendy be in the Science Club? We'd look really good on the telly.'

'Sorry Leanne,' Mr Quayle said. 'You can join the Science Club by all means but I've already selected the team so I'm afraid you won't be on TV. But you're welcome to come along and cheer us. The quiz is being held at the Convention Centre.'

Harriet looked over at Frankie and Frankie grinned back at her. Wendy and Leanne scowled.

At breaktime Frankie volunteered to help put the science equipment away so she wouldn't have to answer Leanne and Wendy's questions about Romeo.

She almost dropped the test tubes she'd just cleaned when she saw Leanne's and Wendy's faces pressed to the window.

'We want to speak to you,' Leanne shouted.

'Soon,' added Wendy.

Frankie ignored them.

The last lesson of the morning was English with Miss Gray.

'Today we're going to begin studying one of Shakespeare's most popular plays,' Miss Gray said. The class-room door swung open.

'Ooh,' said Leanne, from the double desk behind Frankie.

Wendy poked Frankie in the back.

Frankie looked up. Romeo was standing at the class-room door.

'Hey, Frankie!' he said.

'Are you one of the exchange students?' Miss Gray asked, putting her glasses on.

'No, I'm Frankie's boyfriend.' He grinned at Miss Gray. 'Oh I remember you, you were at the disco. You were dancing with a man with a ginger and grey beard. You asked him if he wanted to come back to your place for coffee.'

The room was as quiet as an eclipse, everyone was staring at Romeo. What was he going to say next? Who'd Miss Gray asked back for coffee? The only person with a ginger and grey beard was Mr Hart, the drama teacher.

'How on earth do you know that?' Miss Gray spluttered. 'You couldn't have overheard us with all the noise of the disco.'

'I could, easily. I . . .'

'He's got very good hearing,' Frankie interrupted, fearing he'd tell her about the miniature stereo micro-phone in his ears.

'He must have,' said Miss Gray crossly. She turned back to Romeo. 'What are you doing here?'

'The head teacher said I could visit,' Romeo said.

'Well, take a seat and keep quiet.'

Romeo walked over to the empty seat beside Frankie and sat down.

Frankie scowled at him to show she wasn't pleased to see him. But he only grinned to show that he was *very* pleased to see her.

Miss Gray handed Romeo a copy of *Romeo and Juliet*.

Romeo looked at the cover and then shook Frankie's arm.

'Hey, this book's about me, Frankie!' he said. 'A whole book about me!'

'Have you studied *Romeo and Juliet* before?' Miss Gray asked him.

'No, I've never read this book. But my name's Romeo,' Romeo said. He smiled winningly at Miss Gray, but she didn't smile back.

Romeo turned to the first page and started to read, very fast.

Miss Gray said, 'One of the most famous speeches is of course the balcony –'

Romeo jumped up. 'I know it! I know it!' he shouted.

Miss Gray was too stunned to say anything.

Romeo started to recite Romeo's speech:

'But soft! What light through yonder window breaks . . .' He didn't look once at his book, and the speech was very long, yet he was word perfect. Romeo didn't just say the words. He brought the part to life.

'. . . And then Juliet says: "Ay me" . . . and then we fall in love. But in the end we die. It's so sad.'

For a moment there was total silence in the class. Then Wendy started clapping and everyone, except Miss Gray and Frankie, joined in.

Romeo took a bow.

'I thought you said you hadn't studied *Romeo and Juliet* before,' Miss Gray said suspiciously.

'I haven't.'

'Then how did you know Romeo's speech?'

'I learnt it.'

The rest of the class burst out laughing.

Miss Gray looked grim. 'No one can read a play and instantly be able to recite speeches from it,' she said. 'You've hardly had time to do more than skim through it.'

Romeo looked outraged. 'I did have time. I'm a very fast learner.'

More laughs from the rest of the class. Frankie felt mortified.

'Shut up, Romeo,' she whispered.

Miss Gray looked as if she was about to burst a blood vessel. 'Be quiet!' she yelled.

But the class was in uproar and no one listened. Luckily the bell rang.

'Saved by the bell again,' Frankie thought. She was beginning to like Brentfield's bell very much indeed.

It was lunch break and Frankie had a lot of things to

say to Romeo. She pulled him over to a private corner in the playground.

'What are you doing here? I told you you *couldn't* come to my school.'

'No. You said you didn't want me to go to school *with* you on Monday morning and I didn't go with you. I came on my own.'

'Romeo . . . you know what I meant.'

Romeo looked sorry for himself.

'I just want to learn lots of things and be clever like you,' he said.

'But what if your power management pack runs out again?'

'I brought the spare one and anyway I've been working on a way for the power pack to keep regenerating itself so I won't need to have a spare one soon.'

'But . . .'

'Hello, Romeo,' said Leanne. 'What's that you were saying about power management packs?'

'Just some TV programme we were watching last night,' Frankie lied quickly.

Romeo was about to contradict her but she gave him a look and he didn't say anything.

'We're so glad you're visiting our school,' Wendy said.

'Thank you,' said Romeo. 'I'm very glad to be here even if some people don't seem very pleased to see me.'

Darren came over.

'Hi, Darren,' said Romeo.

'Hi,' said Darren. 'I didn't expect to see you here. Having fun?'

'Yes,' Romeo said. 'I want to come to school every day.'

Darren turned to Frankie and whispered, 'I thought you said there was no way he was coming to our school. Did you change your mind?'

'No. He just turned up. I'd send him home but I'm not sure he'll go and anyway I don't want him wandering around the streets by himself.'

'But it's PE this afternoon.'

'I know. Could you keep an eye on him for me? Please.'

Darren looked at Frankie's worried face. 'I suppose so,' he sighed.

'What's PE?' Romeo asked.

'Sports, games . . . running about, throwing balls.'

'Oh good. I like playing games,' Romeo said. 'What game will we be playing, Frankie?'

'I won't be with you,' Frankie told him. 'Boys have games separately to girls . . .'

Romeo didn't look so happy.

'But Darren will be with you.'

Romeo smiled. 'OK – you and me on the same team, Darren?'

'Sure,' Darren said.

After lunch Romeo went off with Darren to the boys' changing room. Frankie headed off with the other girls for a game of hockey.

'I need a volunteer to miss hockey and do a job for me in the hall,' Miss Myers said.

Frankie's hand went up faster than lightning. Just faster than Meera's.

'Nice to see you so enthusiastic about something for a change, Frankie,' Miss Myers said. 'All right. I want you to tidy up the PE cupboard. It's in a dreadful mess.'

Frankie headed off to the hall, smiling. The PE cupboard, at the side of the hall, looked as if there'd been a small war in it. It was going to take at least all afternoon to sort out. Frankie pulled the door to, but not shut, so that she could watch the boys' PE session, and set to work unscrambling hoops and unravelling sports bands.

A few minutes later her nice quiet cupboard shook with the sound of boys running noisily into the hall. Romeo came in looking like the perfect sportsman in his borrowed PE kit. Darren stumbled in behind him looking dishevelled and worried.

Mr Marks, the PE teacher, looking very muscular, but hairy around the shoulders, in a vest T-shirt, divided the boys into two teams to play basketball. Luckily Romeo and Darren were on the same team, so Darren could show him what to do. Not that he needed much help. Romeo soon got the hang of the game and by the end of ten minutes was playing like someone who'd played it all his life.

Romeo and Darren's team won the first game and

everybody wanted Romeo on their team for the next one.

'I thought you said you hadn't played basketball before?' Mr Marks said. He didn't sound cross. He sounded happy.

'I learn very fast,' Romeo said.

'You're telling me,' said Mr Marks, slapping Romeo on the back.

Everybody wanted Romeo on their team for the next game, but nobody wanted Darren. He hovered at the back trying to look as though he didn't care.

'I only want to play on the team that has my friend Darren in it,' Romeo said.

And suddenly, instead of no one wanting him, a position Frankie could sympathise with, everybody did.

And the team with Romeo and Darren in it won easily.

Mr Marks put an arm around Romeo's shoulders as if they were old friends. 'We could do with you on the school basketball team,' he said.

'Can Darren be in it too?' Romeo asked.

Mr Marks frowned. 'Well . . . I don't know about that.'

'I'd like to be in the team, but only if Darren could be in it too.'

'Hmmm, well, maybe Darren could be the team mascot.'

'OK.'

It was Science Club after school. Frankie and Darren went and Romeo went with them.

Mr Quayle was really excited about the competition. 'I really think we've got a good chance of winning,' he said.

Romeo put his hand up.

'Yes?'

'If we win will we get a cup?'

'No – even better – a shield,' Mr Quayle said. 'And that girl you like, Darren, what was her name? Oh yes – Kookie the Space Warrior – she'll be presenting the prizes.'

'I have to be in this competition too,' Romeo announced. 'I'm really good at science. Ask me a question.'

'Well – I don't know – you're not officially part of this school,' Mr Quayle said.

'Ask me a question – any question,' Romeo insisted, and for the rest of the session he answered correctly the increasingly difficult questions that Mr Quayle threw at him.

'You weren't lying when you said you were good at science,' Mr Quayle said, when it was time to go home. 'Anyone would think you had a computer instead of a brain inside your head.'

'I do,' Romeo said.

'Ha ha,' Frankie and Darren fake-laughed. 'Just his little joke.' They hustled Romeo out of the science lab as quickly as possible.

'I can't believe it,' Darren said, as they walked out of school. 'This is the best day of my life. Not only might we get to meet Kookie but I'm in the school basketball team! Me – Darren Quayle – who's never been in a sports team in his life! Me – the last person to get picked to play anything. I'm in the school basketball team!'

Darren was grinning like a Cheshire cat. He looked as if he could break out in a jig at any moment. Frankie hadn't realised that being in a school sports team could be so important to someone.

'You'll make a great mascot, Darren,' Romeo said.

Frankie didn't say anything. If Darren wanted to be the basketball team's blue and yellow spotted chicken mascot that was up to him. It certainly seemed to be making him happy.

'What's that?' Romeo said, pointing at a dense black cloud, billowing upwards.

'Looks like . . .'

'FIRE!' someone screamed.

The next instant Romeo was racing towards it.

'Stop!' Frankie shouted after him. He didn't stop.

Darren and Frankie ran after him, but Romeo was much faster than they were.

The fire was in a block of flats. People were pointing upwards. Frankie looked up. The smoke was so fierce it made her eyes water. On the top floor a little boy was trapped. No one could reach him. Romeo started to climb up the outside of the building, stretching from window ledge to window ledge. At any moment he could fall. He didn't seem to care about the danger he was in: his one aim was to reach the screaming child above him.

'I hope he doesn't melt,' Frankie said.

'Shouldn't do,' Darren said. 'We sprayed him with that fire retardant stuff.'

'But what if it's worn off – like sunscreen.' No fire retardant could be that strong.

A siren sounded. The fire engine had arrived.

But Romeo had already reached the little boy.

The fire engine's ladder was swiftly raised. The child was now in Romeo's arms. The fire engine ladder stretched towards them. Romeo, holding the boy, stepped onto the ladder and it was lowered to the ground.

'Thank you, thank you!' a woman laughed and cried.

'That's OK,' Romeo said.

The woman took the frightened little boy from him and hugged him to her. A paramedic guided them towards a waiting ambulance.

The press circled Romeo like children in a playground.

'Why did you do it?' one asked.

'Are you a gymnast?' asked another.

'Do you have a death wish?'

'Have you done this sort of thing before?'

'No,' Romeo said.

Camera flashes and clicks filled the air. A local TV news crew pushed a microphone in his face.

'Fire can kill. I didn't want the little boy to die,' Romeo said. 'Anyone would have tried to save him.'

The press didn't agree. Most people would have been too scared of the fire to try and save someone else.

'Did you know the child?' a woman reporter asked.

'No.'

'What school do you go to?'

'Frankie's school.'

'Who's Frankie?'

'My girlfriend.'

'Is she here?'

'Yes, she's over there.' Romeo pointed at Frankie.

The next moment Frankie and Darren were surrounded by press and photographers. It felt intimidating. Frankie didn't like it.

'Let's have a photograph of the two of you together,' a photographer said, pushing Frankie towards Romeo.

'Put your arm around her then,' the photographer ordered Romeo.

Romeo obeyed.

'Kiss him, he's a hero,' the photographer said to Frankie.

Frankie felt embarrassed. She was proud of Romeo. Very proud. But she'd also been very scared that something awful would happen to him. Why couldn't they just let them go home?

'Go on.'

She kissed Romeo on the cheek. His hair smelt of smoke. She was glad he hadn't melted.

'Not like that – like you mean it!' one of the photographers said, sounding disgusted.

'Like this,' Romeo said, and he kissed Frankie as if they were in some slushy movie. The photographers happily snapped away.

10

The whole school seemed to be waiting for them as Frankie, Romeo and Darren walked through the gates the next morning.

'There he is!' Wendy and Leanne cried.

'Saw you on the telly,' said a boy from the year below.

'You were really brave,' said Wendy.

'He was,' Frankie agreed, trying to join in.

'Yeah, saving that kid took guts.'

'Can I have your autograph?' said someone else.

'And me.'

'Write it on my maths book.'

'OK,' Romeo said, and he wrote 'Romeo Chip' wherever people wanted him to.

Wendy and Leanne got him to write it on their hands and then drew a big heart around his name.

The bell rang.

'See you later,' Darren said.

All the way to the first lesson people kept stopping

Romeo to slap him on the back, or high-five him, or just say, 'You're a hero.'

Frankie got a bit tired of it.

'Come on, Romeo,' she said. 'We're going to be late.'

In English Miss Gray no longer looked grimly at Romeo. She smiled.

'I've been telling Mr Hart, the drama teacher, about you. He's looking for someone to play the lead in this year's school play. Will you be staying with Frankie for the next few months?'

'Yes.'

'Oh good. I told him you had all the makings of a fine actor and he wants to see you in the hall at break-time.'

'OK,' Romeo shrugged, as if it was no big deal.

Frankie felt cross. People like *her* auditioned for every school play going and were never even given a walk-on part. And here he was with the lead practically being offered him on a plate. Didn't he knew how lucky he was?

Probably not.

Romeo was busy studying an ant crawling across his desk, unaware of how interested everyone else in the room was in him. He was so unselfconscious. So confident. He just expected everything to work out OK. Just expected everyone to like him. He hadn't been 'alive' long enough to know that life wasn't always that easy.

Frankie wasn't exactly jealous. She just wished

everything could be as easy for her as it was for him.

At breaktime Frankie went with Romeo to the hall. Mr Hart was already there.

'Ah, Romeo, isn't it?' Mr Hart said, straightening his tortoiseshell glasses.

Romeo nodded. He stared at Mr Hart's beard.

'Is that itchy?' he asked.

'What?' said Mr Hart.

'Your beard, is it itchy?'

'No,' Mr Hart smoothed his beard. 'It's soft, not itchy.'

'Can I feel it?'

'I don't think . . .'

'Please, I've never felt a beard before.'

'Oh all right.' Mr Hart looked as if he wished he'd never agreed to audition Romeo.

Romeo tentatively touched Mr Hart's beard.

'You're right – it's soft not itchy,' he said.

'Right, well can we get on now? Frankie, you've had your audition already, haven't you?' Mr Hart said.

'Yes. I . . . I . . .'

'Well, now you're here, maybe you can help Romeo by reading Mina's lines from the scenes I've marked.'

'OK.' Frankie grinned.

Mr Hart gave Romeo and Frankie two pages of script.

Frankie took the pages with slightly shaking hands. Mina's part! A huge part. The best part. The one every girl in the school wanted. This was her chance to impress Mr Hart. Maybe he'd even think that she and Romeo acted so well together that she should be Mina and he should be Dracula.

They went up onto the stage.

'When you're ready,' Mr Hart said.

Romeo put his script down.

'I know it,' he said, and fixed Frankie with a dangerous but sexy Dracula stare. Frankie did her best to portray the shy but strong Mina.

When they'd finished she looked over at Mr Hart. He wasn't looking at her; he was staring at Romeo.

'Mr Hart, sir?' Frankie said.

'Amazing,' Mr Hart said. 'Not only have you got a photographic memory but you could have been made for the part.'

'Me for the part of Mina?' Frankie thought hopefully, but knew she wasn't the one Mr Hart was speaking to.

'I like playing Dracula,' Romeo said. 'Do I get to wear makeup and funny clothes for the play?'

'Oh – er yes,' said Mr Hart. 'Lots of makeup and two fangs and a long black cloak and you swish around and say, "I am the master of the night".'

'When will we know, sir?' Frankie interrupted.

'I'll put a notice outside the hall after school today.'

'Right.'

The bell rang. Time to go back to class. Science next. As they were leaving the hall Mr Hart said, 'Would you mind staying, Romeo? I'd like to go through some more lines.'

'Do you want me to stay too?' Frankie asked, hopefully. 'I could keep reading Mina's lines.'

'No thank you, Frankie.'

Frankie went back to class. She knew she didn't have much chance of getting the part of Mina; Mr Hart would have asked her to stay if she did.

But at least there was the Science Club competition coming up and if she was asked to choose whether she wanted to be a famous scientist or a famous actress she'd pick scientist every time.

'Where's Romeo?' Mr Quayle asked, as soon as Frankie walked in. 'He's not sick is he? It's the competition on Saturday. Dennis has got chickenpox and I want Romeo to take his place.'

'He's fine,' Frankie said. 'He's reading lines with Mr Hart.'

'Did you see Romeo on the news, sir?' Leanne said.

'No,' said Mr Quayle.

'He saved a kid from a burning building.'

'That boy truly is amazing.'

At lunchtime Frankie ended up eating her sandwiches alone, as usual, because Darren and Romeo were off practising for their first basketball game. Even Wendy and Leanne weren't around to ask endless questions about Romeo because they had cheerleader practice.

'Lucky the game's in the hall. It looks like it's going

to rain and I wouldn't want to do my chicken dance in the rain . . . You are going to be there to watch after school, aren't you, Frankie?' Darren said, on his way to get his chicken mascot costume altered.

'Course.'

'Oh good. It wouldn't be the same without you.'

By the end of lunchtime the rain had turned heavy.

'Just my luck,' thought Frankie, miserably. 'Hockey in the rain *all* afternoon.'

But when she got to the changing room Miss Myers was dressed in aerobics gear.

'We're going to have aerobics in the music room instead of hockey today,' she said.

Frankie suddenly felt much happier.

Everyone trooped off to the music room.

'Arrange yourselves so you've got space around you and are facing the front,' Miss Myers said, and she switched on the CD player.

Frankie loved the loud music but found it hard to keep up with the steps.

'Grapevine to the left, star jump, star jump.'

'Ooops, sorry, Harriet.'

'It's to the *left*, Frankie.'

'Grapevine to the right, star jump, star jump.'

'Oops, sorry Leanne.'

'Get off my foot.'

'And march it out.'

'At least you can do the marching right, Frankie.'

'Thanks a lot, Wendy.'

'Your boyfriend's watching us.'

Frankie looked over at the window and saw Romeo looking in. *Her boyfriend* the hero, basketball star, and probably soon to be the lead in the school play. Well, that was what she'd wanted, wasn't it, to make Wendy and Leanne jealous? So how come she wasn't feeling happy? It wasn't Romeo's fault. He'd been all she'd expected and more. Only she wasn't happy. A fake boyfriend wasn't the same as the real thing.

She smiled and waved at Romeo, but he didn't wave back. He frowned.

'Grapevine to the right and kick left,' shouted Miss Myers.

'Oops. Sorry,' said Frankie, who'd kicked right.

'Yeowch!' yelled Leanne, 'Kick me once more and I'll punch you.'

After school Frankie went to the hall to watch the basketball team play against another school called St Matthew's.

Before going in she checked on the noticeboard to see if Mr Hart had put up the list of who was playing which part in the school play. He hadn't.

Frankie found a seat in the middle row and sat down. Around her people were chatting with their friends. She felt very lonely. She tried to pretend she was just waiting for her friends to arrive, but it didn't work.

It seemed to take ages for the whistle to blow and the match to begin. But finally it did and as always

Romeo was the star. St Matthew's didn't stand a chance against Romeo. Wherever Romeo threw the ball from it landed in the basket.

'Ro-me-o! Ro-me-o!' The cheerleaders chanted from one side of the hall.

Darren danced along the other side of the hall dressed as a blue and yellow chicken.

'She can't be his girlfriend,' Frankie heard a girl behind her say, and knew she was being talked about.

'She is,' someone else insisted in a loud whisper.

'What does he see in *her*?'

Frankie's face burned. She wanted to jump up and run home but she'd told Darren she'd wait for him and Romeo. So she sat still and watched the match and pretended she hadn't heard a thing.

Romeo scored another basket.

The cheerleaders went crazy. Darren leapt about doing a wild chicken mascot dance. Frankie was sure that inside the chicken mask Darren was smiling. She smiled too.

After the match the teams went to have their photos taken, along with the cheerleaders and Darren.

The hall emptied and Frankie was left sitting alone. She wondered how long they were going to be. Then she remembered the school play. Mr Hart must have put up the notice by now. She jumped up and went to have a look.

The cast list was written on orange paper and stuck bang in the middle of the noticeboard.

Dracula: Romeo Chip

'What a surprise,' thought Frankie.

Jonathan Harker: Tim Nelson
Van Helsing: Rhys Lennon
Renfield: David Brooker
Mina: Leanne Summers

Of course, thought Frankie. It would be *her*.

'Ready to go?' Darren said, behind her. He'd changed out of his chicken costume.

'Yes.'

'So what part are you playing?'

Frankie pointed to the last line.

All other people who auditioned will play villagers, ship's crews and vampires etc.

Romeo came out of the changing room.

'You got the lead,' Darren told him, slapping him on the back and pointing to his name on the list.

'Good,' Romeo said, but he didn't sound as if he meant it.

'You OK?' Frankie asked.

'Yes,' Romeo shrugged.

Frankie frowned. If he'd been human she'd have said he was sulking or maybe just tired.

Darren hadn't noticed there was anything wrong.

'That was so much fun,' he said, as they walked out of school. 'I can't wait for the next game.'

They were about half way home when Romeo said, 'Your body, Frankie . . .'

Frankie gulped. What about her body? 'Yes?'

'Why isn't it fitter? More toned? Like some of the other girls, like Kookie's?'

Frankie opened her mouth and then closed it again.

'I like Frankie's body,' Darren chipped in loyally.

'Yes,' Romeo said. 'You like all things about Frankie, Darren. And your body is of a similar type to hers. But a boy like me – muscular and handsome – shouldn't I have a muscular and handsome girlfriend – like Leanne or Kookie?'

'Of course not!' Frankie said. 'That's not the way it works.'

'Isn't it?' Romeo said.

'No – it doesn't matter what someone looks like. You have a boyfriend or a girlfriend because you like them and have fun together and can spend hours with each other without getting bored.'

'Like you and Darren?' Romeo said, but he spoke quite softly and Frankie didn't think Darren heard. Or at least she hoped he hadn't. How embarrassing. Romeo was starting to sound like her mum – trying to pair her off with Darren. Didn't anyone realise Darren was just a friend, not a *boyfriend?*

'See you tomorrow,' said Darren, as they came to his turning.

'Bye,' said Frankie.

'Bye,' said Romeo. 'Frankie, when someone tells you to do something do you always have to do it?'

'No. Not if it's something you really don't want to do. Or something that's wrong.'

'But what if your friends don't like you if you don't do what they say?'

'Then they're not proper friends.'

'But what if I do what I think's right and *no one* likes me?'

Frankie grinned. 'There's no risk of that, Romeo. People like you for yourself, not because you *obey* them.'

They'd reached home.

Romeo went down to the basement through the trapdoor.

Frankie went in the front way.

'Hello love. You're back late,' Mum said.

'Yeah. I was watching a basketball match. Darren's the school team's mascot.'

'And you stayed behind to support him. How sweet.'

Frankie didn't feel sweet.

'I'm going down to the basement to do my homework.'

When she unlocked the basement door she caught Romeo busily typing something into the computer.

'What are you doing?'

'Oh, er, nothing. Finished now.' Romeo stood protectively in front of the computer so she couldn't see the screen.

'Were you e-mailing someone?' Frankie knew he must have been. Either that or he was writing the first robot novel.

'No,' Romeo said. But his face gave him away.

'You were e-mailing someone weren't you?' Frankie said.

'Yes.'

'Who? Was it Darren?'

'Darren has e-mail,' Romeo said, but he still looked guilty.

'Romeo . . .'

'Why don't you wear make-up to school like Leanne, Frankie?' Romeo interrupted. 'Or Kookie or Pris?'

'Because I don't want to,' Frankie replied. 'Who were you e-mailing?'

'But your eyelashes would look much bigger with mascara on them. And I like green eyeshadow very much,' Romeo said.

'You wear it then,' Frankie said, through gritted teeth. She was tired of Romeo criticising her. First her body, now her face. What next? 'Now shut up, I've got loads of homework to do.'

'The other boys in the basketball team don't wear make-up,' Romeo said sadly.' But I can wear it when I'm in the school play. Lots of it. Actors are so lucky.'

After school the actors who had speaking parts in *Dracula* went to the hall for a read-through. Frankie wasn't needed.

'See you later,' she said to Romeo, but she wasn't sure if he heard her because he was surrounded by a group of admiring kids – his fan club.

Frankie went to get her books from her locker, but before she reached it she could see there was something stuck to it. As she got closer she saw what it was. A photo of Leanne, looking as smug as a cat who'd eaten the family budgie, with her arms draped around Romeo! Leanne was wearing her cheerleader's uniform. He had on his basketball kit. He should've looked guilty, or at least ashamed of himself, but he didn't. His wide grin was like a taunt.

'Here I am with a suitable girlfriend, who's wearing lots of make-up,' he seemed to be saying to Frankie.

Across the bottom of the photo was written: 'Romeo Chip with his new girlfriend, Leanne Summers.'

Frankie was furious. She ripped the picture off her locker.

Meera and Harriet were coming towards her. They looked as if they wanted to speak to her, but she couldn't speak to them. Frankie turned and ran down the corridor to the hall.

'Frankie!' Meera called.

'Stop!' shouted Harriet.

Frankie didn't stop. She had to see Romeo. Maybe the read-through hadn't started yet.

She pushed open the hall door and ran inside. All the main actors and Mr Hart were seated in a circle. They looked round and stared at her.

'This rehearsal's only for people with speaking parts, Frankie,' Mr Hart said.

Frankie hid the photo behind her back. She couldn't ask Romeo about it in front of everyone. What if he said Leanne *was* his new girlfriend? He'd kept talking about her yesterday.

'Sorry,' she said, and backed out.

'See you later, Frankie,' Romeo said cheerily.

'Yes,' said Frankie. She felt stunned. Betrayed. How could he look so happy and innocent? He was a – a rat! She wished she'd dismantled him after the disco. She'd like to dismantle him right now. Piece by piece until he was nothing but parts!

Meera and Harriet were waiting for her outside the hall.

'I could hit Leanne sometimes,' said Harriet.

'She was all over him,' Meera said. '*Reeeeevolting* girl! It was after the basketball match. We told her to stop but she wouldn't.'

'She only did it because she was jealous of you. It didn't mean anything,' Harriet said.

'Didn't it?' Frankie said. She felt cold and shaky. She wondered if she was going to be sick. She thought the photo meant a lot. She thought it meant even a robot boyfriend she'd made could be more interested in someone else than in her.

'We're going to McDonald's. Come with us,' Meera said. '*Pleeease.*'

'Yeah,' said Harriet. 'Come on.'

Frankie didn't really feel like going, but she went with them, and gradually started to feel better. She even managed not to think about the photo and Leanne and Romeo and what it all meant for a few seconds.

She found she had lots of things in common with Meera and Harriet – including loving Luke Catalan movies.

'There's a new one on at the pictures,' said Meera.

'Let's all go and see it on Saturday,' said Harriet.

'What, all three of us?' said Frankie.

'Course,' said the other two.

They swapped phone numbers so they could talk more about it later.

'Leanne hugging Romeo didn't mean anything,' Harriet said, as they got up to leave.

'No,' Meera agreed. 'You're worth two of her.'

'Lots more than two,' said Harriet. Then she laughed. 'Except on the hockey pitch.'

Frankie walked home, wondering just what the photo did mean. It wasn't as if Romeo was really her boyfriend. He was only a robot, for goodness sake. But that wasn't the reason she was feeling so hurt. It was what everyone else was thinking that hurt like a knife turning. They all thought that she'd loved Romeo and he'd decided that she wasn't good enough for him and had kissed someone else instead. And that person had just happened to be Leanne – the worst person it could possibly be. She'd never let Frankie forget it. Leanne would just relish reminding her at every moment that Romeo had picked her.

When she got down to the basement Romeo was already there, typing something into the computer.

'So what's the meaning of this?' she said, pushing the photo in his face.

Romeo took the photo and glanced at it. He looked back at the computer.

Internet Mail	File Edit View Insert Format Tools Help **SEND**
Inbox: 0 messages Sent Mail: messages	Sender: Romeo Subject: None Time: 18.07
Your message has been sent.	

' "Romeo Chip with his new girlfriend Leanne Summers",' Frankie said, stabbing her finger at the writing underneath the photo. '*Your girlfriend.*'

'Leanne said she should be my girlfriend, not you, Frankie,' he said simply. 'She said I should be seeing someone pretty.'

Hurt, Frankie asked: 'Aren't I pretty?'

'Yes, but you're not – not glossy and made-up like Leanne, or Kookie. Kookie wears lots of make-up.'

'Not glossy! You mean not fake!'

'OK, OK, keep your hair on. I don't know why you're getting so cross. The other boys, not Darren – he was changing out of his chicken costume – but the others, said Leanne liked me and I should kiss her.'

This was getting worse. 'So you did?' Frankie gulped.

'Yes.'

Frankie didn't know what to say. 'Was it nice?'

Romeo shuddered. 'No, horrible. Her lipgloss was all sticky. I thought my lips would get stuck.'

'You shouldn't have kissed her.'

'Why not?'

'Because if you've already got a girlfriend you shouldn't go round kissing someone else. It's not fair.'

'So I have to keep kissing the same person forever?'

'No – but when you don't want to go out with someone any more it's only kind to tell them.'

'OK, Frankie,' Romeo said, and then he dropped his bombshell. 'I don't want you to be my girlfriend, Frankie. I . . .'

Frankie felt like she'd been slapped in the face. She knew what was coming and she didn't want to hear about him and Leanne.

'I wish I'd never made you!' she gasped and ran out of the basement and up the stairs to her bedroom.

Making Romeo had been the biggest mistake of her life. Why did she ever think that a robot boyfriend would be the answer to her problems? How could she have been so stupid?

'You OK, love?' Dad said, as she went past his study.

Frankie stopped. She wanted to tell him. But she'd dug herself in so deep. It'd be hard to explain. Still, it was tempting.

'Why don't I make us a cup of tea?' Dad said.

Frankie nodded. Dad went down to the kitchen and Frankie curled up in his big old office chair. She was looking at the computer and suddenly she knew what she had to do. The person she should have told right at the beginning. She pulled Dad's laptop towards her and pressed e-mail.

'Dear Gran,' she typed.

'I know I should have told you before and I am sorry that I didn't. But you'd better know now. I found a dismantled robot in one of your trunks and I made him, but now I wish I hadn't.

Frankie.'

She'd gone up to her room by the time Dad came back with the tea.

*

It was the Science Club of the Year quiz on Saturday.

Frankie didn't really want to go because she didn't want to spend any more time than she absolutely had to with Romeo. She got ready anyway because she had to go whether she wanted to or not. She couldn't let Mr Quayle down – he was even more excited than the members of the Science Club about the competition. And her mum and dad and most of the guests who were staying at the B&B were coming to watch.

My Quayle picked Frankie and Romeo up in his ancient car that smelt of dogs – even though the Quayles didn't own a dog. Darren and Harriet were already in the car. Romeo sat in the front and Frankie sat in the back, staring at his head. Since the argument she'd hardly said a word to him – although Romeo kept acting as if nothing had happened. Maybe to him nothing had. The only time she'd caught him acting suspiciously was when he was e-mailing someone on the computer. She supposed that the person he was e-mailing was Leanne so she didn't ask about it because she didn't want to hear a word about any lovey-dovey stuff between them.

'All ready?' Mr Quayle said.

'Yes,' said Frankie. 'Mum and Dad are coming along later to watch.'

'Oh good. How about you, Romeo, are your parents coming?'

'I don't have . . .'

Frankie poked him in the back of the neck.

'Ow, Frankie. What did you do that for?' he said.

'His parents can't make it. They've got to work,' Frankie told Mr Quayle.

'Oh right.' Mr Quayle pulled up in the Convention Centre car park. It was busy with students and teachers arriving from other schools. Everyone was dressed in school uniform so that they'd be identified with their school. Romeo was wearing a school uniform that Mr Quayle had found in the lost property box.

The five of them walked into the main hall of the Convention Centre where the quiz was being held. The first few rows had reserved tickets on them for the participating schools.

'Here we are,' said Mr Quayle, as he spotted Brentfield's name in the second row. They sat down to wait until it was their turn to go up on the stage and have questions asked of them by the host, Bertram Brown.

He came onto the stage a few seconds later.

'Welcome, welcome,' Bertram greeted everyone, the cheesy grin that he used when he was hosting his TV programme 'Catch the Word' stuck to his face.

Then the stage manager climbed up onto the stage, holding a clipboard and a walkie talkie, and told them how the whole show would be taped on one day but would be broadcast in segments over the coming weeks.

'It's a head to head with each team being asked twenty minutes of questions. The winning team of each head to head goes on to the next round.'

'What about the losing team?' someone asked.

'They get to sit out and watch the rest of the competition.'

Romeo put his hand up.

'Yes?' said the stage manager.

'Where's Kookie?' he asked.

'She'll be along later to give out the prize to the winning team.'

'That'll be us,' Romeo said, as Frankie pulled him back down into his seat.

'Ssh,' she said.

But of course he was right. The first team they were up against didn't stand a chance and nor did the second.

'We could really win this,' Frankie started thinking.

She saw Mum and Dad sitting in the audience and grinned at them. Earlier they'd made the most of the opportunity to hand out leaflets in the Convention Centre advertising the B&B. Not that they needed much extra advertising. The place was doing really well.

It was time for the semi-finals. They were up against Galliard School.

'What's the atmosphere of Neptune?' Bertram Brown asked.

Frankie pressed her buzzer. 'Mainly methane gas,' she said.

'Correct,' said Bertram Brown.

'We have to win this,' she heard Romeo mutter beside her.

She didn't know what he was so worried for. If they won, great, but if they didn't it wasn't the end of the world.

'Jupiter and Saturn have thick cloudy atmospheres of?'

Darren pressed his buzzer. 'Hydrogen.'

And so it went on.

'The winner is Brentfield,' Bertram Brown announced at the end of twenty minutes.

There was a short break before the final.

'Is Kookie here yet?' Romeo asked the stage manager.

'Yes, she's just getting changed.'

'Can I see her?'

'Sorry, you're not allowed backstage.'

'But I have to see her,' Romeo said, sounding desperate.

'Well, you can't,' said the stage manager, sounding irritated.

'Come on Romeo, let's go and sit down,' Frankie said. She pulled him unwillingly back over to the seats, but he kept looking towards the backstage area. Frankie had never seen him so agitated. 'What's got into you?'

'My girlfriend,' Romeo muttered.

'What?' said Frankie.

'Time for the next round to begin,' Bertram Brown announced.

'Good luck,' Mr Quayle said, as they went back on the stage. 'Make Brentfield proud.'

The questions came thick and fast but Romeo got every one right.

'We did it, Frankie, we won!' said Darren, as the bell sounded for the end of the final.

Frankie smiled at him. It was supposed to have been a team effort but Romeo had answered just about every question this time and would have won even if the rest of them hadn't been there.

Somehow, to her, the victory didn't seem quite as good as when they'd all been answering the questions.

'Where's Kookie?' Romeo said. 'She has to be here to give us our prizes.' He was getting in a state again.

'Calm down,' Frankie told him. 'She'll be here soon.'

And suddenly there she was, looking toned and fit in the leotard thing she always wore, her false eyelashes fluttering.

She shook Harriet's hand first. 'Well done.'

Then Darren's. 'Congratulations.'

'Th-thank you, Kookie,' Darren stammered out.

Then Frankie's and finally Romeo's. Romeo clasped her hand as if he'd never let her go. 'I'm Romeo Chip,' he said. 'Your boyfriend.'

Kookie didn't look pleased. She tried to pull her hand away but Romeo didn't let go.

'Romeo Chip?' she said. 'Aren't you the boy who's been bombarding me with e-mails?'

'Yes. I love you, Kookie,' Romeo said and Frankie had never known him to sound so sincere.

Kookie wasn't impressed. 'Well, I don't love you –

you're a creep, and if you don't stop pestering me with your stupid e-mails I'll be contacting the police.' Suddenly Kookie didn't look so sweet and innocent any more. She wrenched her hand away from Romeo's.

'Maybe you'll learn to love me,' said Romeo. 'I'm very nice once you get to know me.'

Frankie started to feel sorry for him. He'd obviously got a huge crush on Kookie and couldn't understand why she didn't feel the same way back.

'No – I've got a boyfriend I love, thank you very much, and even if I didn't I wouldn't love you. Never ever, not in a million years,' Kookie said cruelly. She stuffed the winners' shield into Romeo's hands. But he threw it to the ground and ran out of the Convention Centre.

For a second, no one said anything, they were too stunned.

Then Frankie said to Kookie; 'What did you have to be so hard on him for? He's just a kid.'

'You don't know what it's like having boys falling in love with you all the time,' Kookie replied, flicking back her hair. 'He had to be told.'

'Huh!' Frankie pushed past her and ran out of the Convention Centre after Romeo but he was far too fast a runner for her to be able to catch him unless he wanted her to. He was down the steps before she had even half opened the exit door.

'Romeo!' she yelled after him, but although she knew he must have heard her he didn't stop.

'Think, Frankie – where'd he head for?' Frankie asked herself. And immediately knew the answer. Home! He'd probably go back to the basement to lick his wounds.

'I'm never going to watch *Kookie the Space Warrior*

again,' Frankie told herself as she ran down to the bottom of the steps and almost bumped into Leanne.

'I suppose you're proud of yourself,' Leanne said. She looked as if she'd been crying.

'What?' said Frankie. She needed to run after Romeo. Not stand around chatting to Leanne and Wendy. And anyway shouldn't *she* be the one who was cross with Leanne? Wasn't Leanne the one who'd stuck the photo on *her* locker? The one who'd stolen *her* boyfriend?

'Romeo said he didn't want to go out with Leanne,' Wendy told Frankie.

'He said it really loudly right in front of *everyone*,' howled Leanne. 'You must have heard about it?'

'No I . . .'

'He said he didn't like the way she kissed him,' Wendy said, with a hint of a smirk on her lips.

'He said he loved someone called Kookie.' Leanne started to sob.

'Oh, I'm sorry,' Frankie said, and she truly did feel sorry for her. Leanne wasn't so bad. 'Don't worry. I bet there's loads of boys who really like you, Leanne . . . and anyway boys aren't *everything*, are they?'

'No – I s'pose not.' Leanne sniffed. She took out a tiny mirror and looked at her tearstained face. Streaks of mascara had run down her cheeks. 'But make-up is!' she shrieked. 'Quick Wendy, back to my place for a retouch. See you on Monday, Frankie.'

Leanne grabbed hold of Wendy's arm.

'Bye, Frankie,' called Wendy, as she was dragged away.

Frankie ran in the other direction. 'Please don't let him be *too* upset,' she wished as she ran up the path to the B&B. Then she stopped. Mum and Dad were standing in the doorway. They'd got here before her – they must have taken the car with them to the quiz.

'Have you seen Romeo?' she gasped. 'I think he was heading this way.'

'D'you mean your friend who got all upset over some girl in a leotard and broke the winning shield when he threw it on the ground?' Dad said.

'Yes.'

'He just went off with your gran and that boyfriend of hers,' Mum said.

'What?!'

'Yes – it was bizarre. We tried to ask her how her holiday went but she wouldn't even stop for a cup of tea. Just said "Where is he?" Then your friend arrived and she grabbed him and drove off,' Dad said.

'Does she know him?' asked Mum.

'Oh no!' Frankie said, and set off running, faster than she'd ever run in her life before, towards Maximilian's flat. This was a disaster. 'Please don't let me be too late, please don't let me be too late,' she repeated over and over again as she gasped and then got a stitch but had to keep running anyway. She kept remembering her e-mail to Gran. She'd said she wished she'd never made him, but she didn't mean it, not really, only what if Gran thought she did?

Frankie raced up the path to Maximilian's and rang the doorbell over and over with one hand and thumped on the door with the other hand. 'Come on, come on, let me in!'

Maximilian opened the door.

'Frankie, what are you . . .'

'Where is he?' she interrupted.

'If you mean . . .'

'Where is he?'

Then Frankie heard a sound coming from the room behind Maximilian and pushed him out of the way. She'd found Romeo.

'Hello Frankie,' he said. 'Your grandmother says she's going to take the pain of Kookie not loving me away.'

'Don't touch him!' Frankie said to Gran.

'I beg your pardon, young lady. This is my robot and I'll do what I like with it,' Gran said.

'It's OK, Frankie,' Romeo said in a small sad voice. 'Kookie doesn't love me and I don't care what happens to me any more.'

'Well I care!' Frankie said. 'And so does Darren and so do a whole lot of other people.' She glowered at Gran, knowing that if she'd been just a few seconds later Gran might have started dismantling him.

'Sometimes I think you're as silly as your father, Frankie,' Gran said, and pulled up Romeo's shirt to undo his belly button and remove the power pack. 'He's just a robot.'

'Stop!'

'Give me one good reason why I should,' Gran said.

So Frankie did.

'You don't think I opened just the *one* trunk do you?' she said.

Slowly Gran lowered the screwdriver and turned to look at her.

'I couldn't find the keys but fortunately there's lots of hammers and screwdrivers at our place,' Frankie continued. 'It wasn't too hard to break into the smaller trunks. And guess what I found?'

'What?' said Romeo.

'Nothing,' Frankie said, answering Romeo's question but looking at Gran. 'The thing that was inside them had already been made. Hadn't it, Maximilian?'

'Celia?' Maximilian almost squeaked at Gran. 'She knows I'm a robot.'

'You're a robot too!' said Romeo. 'A robot like me?' He was looking at Maximilian with excitement and awe, quite forgetting doom and gloom and wanting to be taken apart.

'Yes, he's a robot too,' Frankie said.

'How did you guess?' Gran asked.

'It wasn't so hard, not once I started thinking about it. Mum never trusted Maximilian. She didn't like the way he just appeared one day out of nowhere and never once spoke about his past – almost as if he didn't have one. I suppose you even bought this flat and then pretended it was Maximilian's.'

Gran sank onto the sofa. 'I'm glad you know,' she said. 'It was so hard never being able to tell anyone. Maximilian was the last thing your grandfather and I made together. He told me to carry on with it if . anything happened to him – so I did and with a little training he became the perfect companion. He couldn't take the place of your grandfather, of course, but he did help me to feel a little less lonely.'

'What about me?' Romeo asked.

'Oh – you were an earlier attempt,' Gran told him.

'I can't let you dismantle Romeo,' Frankie said. 'It'd be like letting you kill a member of my family.'

'But you said in your e-mail you wished you'd never made him.'

'I know. But I didn't mean it. I was just angry. He didn't make a very good boyfriend but I still love him as a friend or a brother.'

'But there'll be too many questions if we let him continue. He's bound to make a mistake,' Gran said. 'You didn't train him properly. The safest thing would be to dismantle him and put him back in the trunk.'

'But you're home now, you can help me. And I didn't do too badly. He seems pretty much like any other teenage boy to me. Human teenage boys are always pretty confused and getting crushes on girls they shouldn't have.'

'Frankie, I don't think you've thought this through. Someone is going to ask where he comes from, who his parents are. I'm amazed you got away with it for the short time you have. You can't expect to keep him hidden away for ever.'

'I'm not thinking of doing that,' Frankie said. 'Not any more. Look at Maximilian and Romeo – see how alike they are. They could easily pass as part of the same family.'

Maximilian and Romeo looked each other up and down. They were very alike and could have been father and son or uncle and nephew.

'So?' said Gran.

'So we use the similarity,' Frankie said. 'We tell everyone that Romeo's Maximilian's nephew. Not only will it help Romeo but it'll help Maximilian too. He'll be part of a real family and so less suspicious than just someone who appeared out of nowhere. Romeo could even stay here if it'd make you happier than him living in the basement.'

'But I like living with you, Frankie,' said Romeo.

'Or he could stay at ours,' Frankie said. 'Only this time we make it official. He'll be a guest with his own room.'

'Your parents would never agree to it.'

'Yes they would. You know they would. They'd agree to anything, especially if you stopped criticising them and saying how the B&B will never work. And we have to tell Mum and Dad the truth about Maximilian and

Romeo. It's not fair to keep this big a secret from them.'

Gran was silent for a few seconds. Then she said, 'I suppose it could work. I'd be able to iron out any problems, even make Romeo mature as he gets older.'

'Now you're getting the idea,' said Frankie.

'You know, you sometimes remind me a lot of myself,' Gran said to Frankie.

'Thank you,' Frankie said, and they smiled at each other.

It was time to tell Mum and Dad.

Gran drove the four of them round down to the B&B. Mum and Dad came running out to greet them.

'What's got into them?' Gran said.

'Remember to be nice,' said Frankie.

'You'll never believe it,' Dad said, pulling open Frankie's door.

'What?' said Frankie.

'My book – the one that got turned down by fifteen publishers – they're going to make it into a film.'

'I've always wanted to be in a film,' said Romeo, admiring himself in the wing mirror.

Dad either didn't hear or decided to ignore him.

'I knew you could do it, Dad,' said Frankie, climbing out of the car to hug him.

'What's this book of yours about?' said Gran, getting out too.

'It's about robots,' said Dad. 'Robots that look exactly like people.'

'Doesn't sound very realistic to me,' Gran said and then she winked at Frankie. 'But I'm sure it'll do very well.'

Dad blushed beetroot. 'Do you mean it?'

Gran nodded.

'We've got a story of our own to tell you about robots,' Frankie said.

'Have you?'

'Yes,' said Gran, linking arms with a surprised Mum. 'Perhaps we'd better go inside.'

'And I'll tell you all about it,' said Frankie.

FRANKIE'S ROMEO

Ruth Louise Symes now lives in London, but has also lived in America, Israel, Singapore, Australia and New Zealand. Some of her jobs have included teaching children with special needs, instructing aerobics, acting in a Chinese soap opera and playing the part of Jill Goose in the pantomime Mother Goose. She has never tried to make a robot but thinks that having one to help tidy up and do the washing up would be very nice.